# *Passionate Encounters*

# *Passionate Encounters*
## Shireen Jabry

# Passionate Encounters

iUniverse books may be ordered through booksellers or by contacting:

iUniverse
1663 Liberty Drive
Bloomington, IN 47403
www.iuniverse.com
1-800-Authors (1-800-288-4677)

Because of the dynamic nature of the Internet, any Web addresses or links contained in this book may have changed since publication and may no longer be valid. The views expressed in this work are solely those of the author and do not necessarily reflect the views of the publisher, and the publisher hereby disclaims any responsibility for them.

ISBN: 978-1-4502-7255-1 (sc)
ISBN: 978-1-4502-7257-5 (ebook)
ISBN: 978-1-4502-7256-8 (dj)

Printed in the United States of America

iUniverse rev. date: 11/09/2010

*Let your soul exalt your reason to the
height of passion; that it may sing;
And let it direct your passion with reason,
That your passion may live through its
Own daily resurrection, and like the
Phoenix rise above its own ashes.*

Khalil Gibran
*The Prophet*

# Contents

# Preface

"So, why are you still complaining? I don't get you. You got what you wanted, and suddenly it's not enough?"

She was my best friend, the one that kept me at bay. You know: the kind that keeps you responsible and sensible.

"It's not enough … not now."

"What is it with you? You're never satisfied."

"The day I'm satisfied is the day I will stop moving up, and …"

"And what? Just explain to me …"

"I'm not even close to where I need to be, so when the day comes, I will be satisfied."

"No, Sara. Don't forget you can't bullshit me. It's me …"

Yeah, that was my best friend. She knew me more than I knew myself.

"OK, fine." I chuckled. "Big deal. So I'm not going to be satisfied that easily—maybe that's my asset right there. Maybe without that I wouldn't be determined."

"Sara," she said. Her eyes used to stare at me, as if they could read all my thoughts, even the ones I was just creating. "That's no way to live your life."

"It's my way." We both said it at the same exact moment.

It was times like this that today, being so far away from then, I miss the most.

I leaned back in my chair at the café and held on to my cappuccino, which had served me and my best friend in all our talks of life, from childhood through adolescence and into preadulthood.

"Not everything can be your way. You know that more than anyone I know, but I still can't figure out why you're afraid of accepting that. So why?"

"I just want too much. I don't know any other way. When it comes to what makes my world go around, I want it all. I need it all."

"Sara, we've been here before. It's not just with your career, it's with everything else, and I've been trying my hardest to make you see that."

"Come on; it's my career." There was a pause. "Don't begin all of this again."

It was always like her. It was like she was following a manual, the *How to Know Sara in Every Detail and in Any Situation Manual*. Perhaps it was simple. We grew up together; perhaps that was enough.

"You're unbelievable."

Laughing and with a smile as broad as daylight, I said, "You're damn right there, and thanks for the compliment. I've always been unbelievable."

"Sara," she laughed, "I miss you; really I do. Maybe, just maybe …"

Tears filled my eyes. My cheeks grew warm, and I stared down at my mug of cappuccino.

"I can't. I can't …"

When I looked up, there was an empty chair in front of me. My tears continued running down my cheeks, and there was nothing.

I finally understood the meaning of feeling empty.

*It was a book I needed to rewrite and the only one I couldn't.*

# Take One

Souls connecting,
Lingering on…
Others are leaving.

Melodies of bodies,
His and hers,
Coming together in unity and harmony.

CREATE, (pause)
A passion,
A thirst of two bodies lurking in each other's keeping.

Tenderness,
A gentle breeze that tickles your senses BLIND.

(Pause) Heat in your words and
            actions…………………………………

A delicate whisper tingles you ears,
*"Who are you?"*
It asks.

And then (Pause) your response spoken from a dialogue
    in your eyes.

Blurred vision,
Tears (pause),
And you're finally home in the arms of your lover.

A voice can be heard,
Shaking in the distance............
*"When a child is born into this world,*
*It has no concept of the melody in its character..."*

Suddenly, a desperate scream escapes the breathless
    horizon,
Demanding to know,
*"(Exactly) who creates that melody?"*

# Take Two

Warmness filled my soul. My hand reached out, stretching to encounter that magical haunt known to mankind.

My fingers preached their existence, hanging on, waiting to feel the warmth of a man's hand.

He stared at me. Just quite simply stood in front of me and continued in his staring saga.

His eyes intense, clouded with the vision of a woman he had loved all these years.

A statue of a man in love.

His shadow filtered through my own, his heart full of bitterness at a love stolen from him.

Seconds gave way to minutes.

I began sweating out the history of our past love.

The memorable moments of two human souls chained together through life's hardships.

The complete indulgence of two characters, hand in hand, protecting each other.

A protection of the heart and mind; a protection of a love that knows no boundaries.

Genuine and bullheaded, I kept my arm stretched out to that man, who had taught me the lesson of love.

That boy, full of energy, full of sympathy to all people around him.

Abruptly, he began to cry.

He drowned in his tears.

Jumping in after him, I swam in his sorrows until I found him and brought him back up for fresher air and a newer beginning.

I rescued a man who had spent almost two years of his life rescuing me.

# Take Three

We took a walk down memory lane.

A walk guided with the legs of the past and the haunting heart of dependability.

I strolled in Kew Gardens, overlooking that same river.

Strolled alongside the reflection of a full moon.

The moon fell out of the sky and dove into the river. I watched that serene moon, gradually drew to a halt, and stood in front of the river.

Closing my eyes, I flew back in a time machine to my past.

I arrived, strolling alongside that same river at 2:00 in the morning.

The morning of September 27, 1998.

"Well," he said, and drew to a complete halt in front of me.

"Which door are you going to open, and which will you shut forever?" he asked with the glimmer of suspense and curiosity in his eyes.

A pause.

A few minutes later, I turned to face him and gave him the answer that would change both of our lives forever.

"I will open the door that is standing in front of me now," I whispered in his ear.

I peered into his face and at once saw the face of a charming man welcome me into his territory.

He turned away and faced the river; I was beside him.

Hand in hand, we stood searching the river for the growth of a friendship that had landed us in lover's land.

"You are the only moon that lights up this night," he said, with compassion in his words.

Smiling, I faced him and kissed him on the cheek.

He hugged me like there was no tomorrow.

"You are the river without which the moon could not be reflected," I whispered delicately in his ear.

And with that, we began our journey alongside the river of expectations.

# Take Four

I ran away, hiding in the only place that I could.

I chose a garden alongside the river in Wimbledon.

This little savior was shielded behind a wall of bricks.

Walking into the little garden, I christened it with my plight.

The brick wall appealed to my nature; it ironically symbolized my fear of hurt.

Although the night was rather chilly, I felt a fire of warmth insulate my heart.

Crying, I realized that he had taken away my happiness, replacing it with emptiness.

No matter where I hid, his presence would lurk in all my venues of refuge.

After all, he was the air that I breathed into my lungs.

The aroma that filled my heart with a difference, a joy, a ludicrous happiness that I had neglected.

"Sorry" was a word that never escaped my lips.

Crying bitterly, I knew I needed to admit my mistake to the only man who believed that I could never make a mistake.

And that's the story of how I learned the lesson of apology.

# Take Five

The irony of the situation drove me to despair.

He had played with me, toyed with my emotions, shattered my beliefs, and fought a battle with my destiny.

As a puppet master, he had encaged his prey, choosing carelessly when to jerk me around.

He had me kicking when he saw fit, had me hugging him when he needed it, had me angry when he chose to display my karate punches to the public.

A puppet I became, as he molded me into that role.

Enraged, I cried tears of a woman scorned.

A woman now in love with a boy of intolerable cruelty.

He faced me wearing the mask of the confused victim.

Reaching for my hand, he showered it with kisses of a time gone by.

Hugging me, he was drenched in the coldness of my icy igloo that had then temporarily replaced my heart.

Uncomfortable, he drastically pulled back.

Questioning my uncharacteristic actions, he dwelled in the house of cheaters before him.

Anger exploded in him, as he briskly welcomed the new novel he had written.

It starred him in the role of a poor, intelligent boy in love with the charms of an innocent angel who had cheated on him, causing his life to crumble around him.

He demanded that I play the role of the cheater, although this was remarkably strange, as I did not know how.

He refused to give me the skills of a cheater, claiming that I had them inbred in my character already.

Laughing, I faced the ridiculous boy who had created a lie and believed his own lie.

Smirking in his face, I withdrew, leaving behind a boy of considerable stupidity guided by his influential friends.

# Take Six

I held the hand of a man who lived a life of imagination.

He breathed the air of a nonexistent society.

He smelled the aromas of characters that he cheekily invented.

He touched the life of the woman who had her nose always buried in a novel.

He smiled in reassurance to a woman who had spent her life dreaming and her wakeful hours recalling the exact details of her dream.

She recorded her dreams, throwing away her reality.

She lived a life of breaks inhabited in the land of her dreams.

She smiled in reassurance to a man who spent his life dreaming of centuries, of stories untold, and of people unheard of.

She unknowingly tickled the senses of a man who saw his mind reflected in the glow of her eyes.

They walked on, hand in hand, exchanging stories, borrowing some, buying others, until the day that others that walked this earth acknowledged their intelligence.

Sleeping, she awoke to the sweet, delicate ring of her mobile that captured the voice of her lover.

Muttering into the handset, she heard his laughter as he honored her voice when he was the first to hear it every morning.

She sent him to his dreams, night after night, wishing him farewell into a land of considerable delights mirrored in perfection.

He sent her to her own dreams, magically reappearing in hers night after night. A reliable asset in her dreams, he fulfilled her heart's desire, only for her to wake up every morning and realize that he was fulfilling her reality as well.

That was when she knew she could not live without the presence of this man in her dreams, this man in her reality, and this man in her life.

She picked up the phone to call him and then, with the first ring, hung up.

She saw no logic in only hearing his voice if she could see his face as well.

And that was the face she was waiting for today.

# Take Seven

He lay in his bed dreaming.

He saw a picture of a river accompanied with beautiful scenery of nature.

Waterfalls were used to water the roses that gave out their sweet, intoxicating scent.

People walked alongside that river, lost to the intensity of their own emotions.

He saw a girl in the distance.

As she walked by him, he suddenly realized that she was a woman.

No longer a girl, she had matured into the woman who had previously massaged his heart back to life, back to its joy.

He wept silently, as he was now a man of strength who was haunted with a weakness for a woman who had touched his soul in ways unimaginable, not to mention unrealistic.

His head hung low, his back arched, he shielded the striking brightness of the summer sun.

He only knew too well the shadow of his joy.

He starved for the day that he would know the joy of a dancing heart among friends, among colleagues at work, and among that woman who gave birth to his joy.

Turning away, he missed the chance he had been waiting for.

The same woman who had passed a few minutes ago stood behind him, a meter and a half away, staring at the arched back of a boy she once knew.

Bewildered, she stood staring at the boy who had made her life worth living. And still makes her life worth living.

But blurred by the magnitude of her memories, she could not tell whether she was staring at the back of the boy, or the man who had now so elegantly replaced him.

She kept her distance, as she clearly saw that man was soaked in considerable worries.

She waited, barely budging an inch for almost an hour, as she watched him.

She closed her eyes, prying into the essence of his depression, the essence of his tears.

But she could not—could not talk to him again, nearly six years after she had deserted him.

Clearly, her presence in his life again would only serve as a reminder of his hurt in the past.

So, with considerable vulnerability, she continued along her journey, this time never stopping to look at whom she passed by.

That man, still and emotional, remained with his head hung low, his back arched; he continued shielding the striking brightness of the summer sun until this day.

# Take Eight

I bit my lip.

Worried, I walked the whole floor of my bedroom at least ten times.

Smothered in the delusion of his absence, I fidgeted with my hair and lips and continued to march back and forth across the room, as if I had been appointed to join the Nazi Gestapo police force.

I suddenly stopped short.

Pausing … to hear whether the phone had rung with news of his whereabouts.

I realized that I was dreaming of the constant ringing tone of my phone.

Worry changed into anger, and anger gave rise to carelessness.

I could not care anymore.

I had had enough of his pathetic problems that he chose to burden me with.

I was burdened with all his problems as he let them out of his mouth, gushing like the water out of a cold-water tap.

I was the one who would caress his worries, putting them to induced sleep, while I took care of his feelings, which were often neglected by most people around him.

In turn he remained aloof, a stranger to me who had chosen to carelessly hide behind my sympathetic nature.

I didn't mind hiding him, but I had minded that he built himself a little mountain on which he proceeded to build a castle, where again he chose to crown himself as a prince.

This mountain was built on a land he did not own, and I was represented symbolically as that land.

He indulged himself with the garden of desires, watering those that would spring up to quench his thirst.

Never a believer in that piece of land, he showered his silence on its soil.

He loved her, that land that would surpass his depression, and he would smirk in the saddening glow of that face.

He had a passion with the land that wrapped him up warm, promising to smother him with security.

He had felt alive.

He could finally relive the years that had been abruptly stolen from him, many years back.

Only now he had neglected the land that diminished his loneliness, that gave birth to his joy, and that protected him from himself.

A dreary, depressed man that nobody cared to help, that people neglected, and that lived a life of denial.

And I was here, worrying about his whimsical, careless whereabouts, his sudden disappearance from my life and his friend's lives.

I envisioned him far away, driving away in a car along a highway to a world only he understood, to another land he would inhabit with his worries and another woman he would caress with the words of his wit.

I chuckled, choked into a sob.

I was relieved that the land was returned to its rightful owner and the garden returned to the cares of a woman that knew not the glimmer of despair in life.

That woman had now finally stopped pacing back and forth in anguish and lustful worry.

The phone started to ring and she came close to it, carried the handset and placed it on her lap, and refused to pick up his call.

It was him, and with that she just as carelessly chose to neglect the man who had taught her how to neglect people by neglecting her.

# Take Nine

He responded in the manner she had dreamed of.

He had written the sentence she longed to hear from a man that would live beside her, sharing her life in all its complexities.

He had read her mind and prescribed the medication that she craved to hear from a man's lips.

He had uttered the words of a lover in the making.

Although he was not yet her partner in the passion crusade that would take residence in her body.

He proved to her his potential.

He filled her days with delight and reminded her how to laugh in the face of her problems and how to rejoice in sharing her moments, whether harsh or kind, meaningful or not, shallow or deep, good or bad, stamped with the seal of boredom or the seal of ecstasy.

She smiled and at once felt at home with a man; she had tiptoed around his heart almost three years back.

She circled his heart at that time, not daring to question the reasoning behind her doubts.

Now, she questioned her life without his love.

Now, she wanted to jump, dive into the ocean of his heart, unafraid of the thrashing, cold waters she could find, or the gentle waves of ecstasy she could swim through.

She glided through her days with his presence in her mind, and her soul grinned. For finally, she had been awarded the Statue of Liberty.

Smoking the true essence of her life, she glowed in ways she only felt once before.

She had also rescued him from the drowning effects of a hurricane of a past love.

A love that he had consumed and re-consumed to the point of destruction.

That woman that he remembered as a girl, sitting in front of him, drinking her daily mug of hot chocolate.

That woman that he wanted to desperately share his life with.

That woman now returned.

Carrying a basket of flavors he would thrive on.

He in turn carried with him a basket of future ventures of passion and compassion.

The basket was made out of the most dependable and reliable material there was around.

Time would tell the story of the exchange of baskets and the trading of two hearts.

# Take Ten

Desperate, he held on to my sleeve.

Pleading with me to reveal the secrets of my past.

The secrets of my heart.

I could never reveal the rivers, which gave into the lake that gave into the oceans of my heart.

A woman's heart was indeed a treasure of experiences.

A treasure she fought to maintain in its glamour. Each jewel, each diamond, and all the pearls of the ocean were carefully handpicked with the knowledge that each ornament had empowered her life in ways unheard of.

The rubies lay scattered among the endless stream of innocent pearls, the diamonds shadowing their counterparts; the gold bracelets, necklaces, and rings.

Among the pile, smack right in the middle, lay a solitaire: a beautiful, sparkling solitaire that glistened, its stones shimmering in an old flame of the past.

A special flame that haunted the center of the woman's heart—the center point that all other treasures were measured against.

The solitaire: every man's worry and concern.

Afraid, men felt mortified with the power of a solitaire.

The power that first love radiated on that girl, teaching her, guiding her with experiments she only imagined.

The solitaire: it sparkled in the eyes of men everywhere, an eclipse that only appeared once every hundred years.

And that was their exact concern.

They could never live up to the shiny radiance of a love unlike any other, of a love that christened their women for the very first time.

Their manhood at risk, they ran away from real women, searching for girls that still knew nothing, experienced nothing.

The girls they encountered were of a considerable young age, their only experience their birth from their womb.

Babies at heart, they won the love of older men who sought women who had never known themselves in love before.

The man taught her how to behave, react, and endure in a life where he again crowned himself her solitaire amid a treasure box filled with emptiness.

He was her only ornament, her only treasure, but demanded that she pretend that he was the center of her universe, although she was too young to have a universe, and he even handed her a treasure box of denial.

And so he pleaded with me.

Pleaded with me to put his mind to rest.

To reveal to him that he was indeed my solitaire, amid a wreck of boyfriends.

I smiled mischievously at that man, who had descended into a boy in my eyes, and turned away from his gaze.

Yanking my arm harshly from his grip, I stepped out of the car, never looking back.

Never looking back at a childish boy who had never even made it to the treasure box.

# Take Eleven

I watched him behind my window.

Watched him play with the kids in the playground.

I wished onto him what God wished upon me.

What God almighty had cornered me with.

He registered me in the tiny corner of talent.

He blessed me with words that engraved my feelings into the magical thresholds of paper.

I cried the tears of success and the stolen heart of a lover.

Emotional, I grew concerned with others that walked along my path in life.

Undoubtedly, the brightest of them is my brother.

Again,

I watched him behind my door.

Peering into the keyhole, I could just about see him running along the road carelessly.

As luck would have it, there were no cars for miles around.

He never admitted any mistake. A doctor in disguise, he hid away from the faults of men by treating men.

Timid and shy, he chose to display a dummy of his strength to his only sister.

Again,

That sister now watched him behind her garden gate.

She smiled at the young man who winked in her direction.

His hair a mess of curls, his face good-looking, his lifestyle overtly serious.

He came closer to her—hugged her—and she hugged him back.

He had gifted her with a hug, a present he seldom ever expressed.

She played with his hair and play-boxed him back to his childhood.

Reserved, he relented, moving back, retorting some medical jargon.

She laughed at the man in front of her that to this day felt a desperate need to hide behind his profession.

Again,

She imagined him screaming at her when he was back home, arguing about everything and nothing at the same time.

She fell over laughing as the irony of her reality came alive.

Her brother hid behind his medical profession, and,

All the while,

She had hid behind her laptop, drowned in the powerful grip of words and desperately trying to build novels of all sizes, burying herself in them.

It was ironic, she realized; indeed, it was very ironic, as she yet

Again, she watched kids—her kids playing in the playground with his.

# Take Twelve

She never knew why she had acted that way, but she always knew enough to know that she was right.

It wasn't until she smelled the scent of his aftershave that it happened.

He was busy chit-chattering about his everyday musings while she lay on the bed staring at him.

He was the humane version of the hustle and bustle of city life, and she knew that's what she loved about him the most.

He never seemed to know when to stop. And to her, that was an aphrodisiac.

Until the moment he completely forgot about her—just sitting there on his bed.

He was the typical man, self-involved and liberated by his sense of pride. She was a typical woman, self-involved but liberated in his presence.

But today, he was just too far out of reach. He was lurking behind a cloud, so far up in the sky that even her desire to find him would be impossible.

So she continued watching him, waiting to be heard and, of course, to be seen. That was the day he lost his sight and, soon after, her voice.

She never knew why she had acted that way, but she knew enough to know that she was right.

As passive as she may have appeared, she was right.

# Take Thirteen

He grew serene, his face hidden in the shadow of a dim light.

He spoke words that jolted my heart into full swing.

Words that read of a story between a man and his woman.

Words that told the sorrows of their pain, the happiness of their joy, and the celebration of their memories.

He kept his face half covered in darkness.

Tilting his head sideways, he moved an inch to cover both his eyes from my view.

I felt an ache that threatened to reopen the wounds of a heart numbed by overexposure.

Stillness gripped the night, cuddling it; the moon rocked the night in its arms, winking in my eyes.

The moon gave me hope, escorted me to a safer threshold, where the Lip-Faced Man could not enter.

He began to speak.

I stood mesmerized, surprised and disturbed.

The man finally spoke, mouthed words.

My eyes fell upon his moving lips.

But I could not hear the words as he spoke them or pronounced them.

Strangled in my realization, I tried to decipher his coded lips, firmly believing that reading lips was an art anybody could master.

He continued his speech.

His mouth moved at an incredible speed.

At times very fast; at other times slow.

He paused.

And again began the speech of curiosity.

I could feel the beating of his lips against each other as he showered me with his spit.

But still nothing.

No voice could be heard.

I looked up desperately at the moon.

The moon played with the darkness that overshadowed part of his circle, to deliver unto me the following message:

"Destiny is in seeing what you believe in and not in hearing what you wouldn't believe."

I had become as serene as the night sky.

# Take Fourteen

I never knew that I could have rocked your heart back and forth violently.

That I could have caused you hurt so deep that it numbed part of your heart.

Years, many years later, I smile in recognition of a love that we both endured with the light of a flame unknown to mankind.

The love that set our hearts aflame with passion and a desire that secured our lives in ways unimaginable.

In memory of our love, you are the pivot on which the balance is attached.

Serene, genuine, and a genius—not in your inventions, but in romance, in your passionate embrace, in your compassion that moves mountains and drains water from the ocean—in being just you.

Almost a decade later, and at nineteen, you were a man before a boy.

In uniting with your best friend, you became a man in your patience, in your dependable character of sincerity, in your tolerance of a love that crucified you as well as crowned you king.

We walked the path of destiny for approximately two of our twenty-six years alive.

That path, until this day, is intoxicated with the most revitalizing flowers, arrangements of the sweetest, most elegantly scented roses, inhabited with the most intensely electrifying moments of our lives.

Enduring our love, we cast a hurricane at those dearest to us. We rained a strong wind of defiance on any person who questioned our love for another.

Failing to realize that those dearest to us only wanted what was best for us in light of their own experiences and beliefs.

Ironically, in that passage of time, we never understood our parents' well-coded language.

Now, and with the cold, piercing shower of maturity, I know the reason for their elusive, strict behavior, their mistrust of a relationship that they somehow failed to wreck.

Believing that our love was like a ship of adventure for youngsters, they tried one too many times to pull the ship back to harbor.

And when all else failed and the titanic ship remained rooted and solid, they jumped into using the might of their words, highlighting even the weapons hidden behind their shields.

Each family threw down their shields and struck while the iron was hot, where it hurt most.

As they struck, their prime attempt was to strip the other family from its historic pride and respect.

Never halting even once to realize that their actions bore resemblance to hunters, hunting for their prey.

The reason why comprehending our love was blindly impossible was simple: our bull-horned resistance to yield to their demands, our consumption with one another, both crucified and crowned us as counterparts: king and queen.

Our parents weren't sailors upon that ship, and they never spent the good hours of their days climbing the rockiest yet most seductive of mountains. Instead, they succumbed, even surrendered, to what they had been taught to parrot in their childhoods.

Tears stinging my eyes, I surrendered to the man of my past.

I surrendered to our memories, and as I walked across my bedroom lost in thoughts of a past unlike any other, I caught a glimpse of myself in the mirror.

That's when it hit me: the importance of loving a boy who became a man before he became a boy.

My first love consumed me and purified me.

It purified love in my eyes, placed heaven on earth, and leapt out of its past to hug me with its smothering warmth.

The warmth that contributed to the woman I became.

And with that, I finally, years later, bid my first love its farewell.

As an afterthought, I sent him a kiss of forgiveness, a kiss of sacrifice, and a kiss from his ex-partner.

# Take Fifteen

I read the valuable document.

It was sealed with the un-forbidden love of the past.

The document gave life to my soul.

It injected me with the bitter dose of reality and swept my soul off into the past.

Rejection never an option, I recalled the delirious, ludicrous, happiest days of my life.

The easiness of a lover's hand cleverly intertwined in my own; the reassuring warmth of his hug; the seductive smile that tickled his lips into frenzy.

The glow in his eyes.

His faith in me, mirrored in his eyes.

My faith in him, mirrored in my day-to-day actions and reactions.

Simply put, his happiness flowed over mine like a waterfall.

His sadness was filtered in my heart.

His excitement sent my adrenaline into full swing.

For he was my twin, my lover, and my friend.

# Take Sixteen

The first boy to enter the cloudy heart of my soul entered stealthily, taking residence in a dark corner and hiding away from the light of life.

That corner was the corner that belonged to the Lost & Found Department.

He assembled the thoughts that were scattered in this area; he had entered a haven of confusion and utter disarray.

Words were spray-painted on the banner hung outside the department, and further anecdotes were engraved into the wooden counter that housed the papers of a life gone by, amid papers of a future yet to be unraveled.

Overjoyed with the clever, witty remarks spray-painted on the banner, he laughed, remembering a boy he once knew.

Caressing with his fingers the endless stream of words engraved with passion on the counter, he grew astonished.

Amazed that a girl who had crossed his path numerous times over the last five months had been, all along, a member of his team of ingenuity and spontaneity.

Charmed, he fell into the chair behind the counter—just for a minute, to catch his breath.

He was very tired, as he was persistent in entertaining ideas that provoked the people he disliked the most.

Falling into the chair, he was welcomed with the comfort of a bed designed especially for his needs. Calmness, like the enchanting waves of the ocean, inhabited his whole being. The softness of the pillows of the chair broke his fall as he absorbed their warmth and compassion.

Closing his eyes, he gradually and easily fell into a sleep, a trance.

That was exactly when he dreamed of a love, a sacrifice: in short, a chance encounter between two souls.

He had felt the vibrations of her heart as she played them into a tune of harmony and elegance.

Her music echoed in the walls of his heart.

He trembled in her embrace, shivering with ecstatic love for a girl that once wore the mask of his best friend.

She smiled when she saw him from a distance.

Knowing very well that he carried her parcel of happiness in his rucksack.

He ran skipping into her arms, hugging her back to life, smothering her with words intricately designed from his love for her and, bouncing up together, they dived into their own world—of course, they were both such vibrant, strange characters that they dived in headfirst.

Hurt from the fall, they both scrambled to their feet, one tending to the other.

It was the very first time she felt pain unlike any she had ever known. A slight pain, packaged with comfort, met her head.

Suddenly feeling overwhelmed with the presence of her heart, she relented, giving her heart to the boy next to her.

At once, he swore that he would live out his days protecting his heart.

Taken aback, she withdrew from the boy, demanding:

"Why have you neglected my heart, only thinking of your own?"

Falling into fits of laughter, he blurted out the truth:

"The heart you gave me is as dear and precious to me as my own. That's why I did not refer to it as yours."

Smiling with relief, she winked at the boy who had won her love with his bubbling wit.

She held his hand and kissed her own.

As he stood watching her plant a peck on the back of her hand with the careful consideration of a woman in love, he felt the gentle peck tickle his skin.

Soon after, they tiptoed around university in one footprint.

Abruptly, he awoke from his favorite dream.

Looking around, he was in the chair behind that wooden counter.

He stood up and walked outside. He mouthed the words that towered above him on the banner hanging outside the department:

"The end."

It was again spray-painted on that banner.

She had reminded him of that boy he once knew.

She had reminded him of himself.

Glancing at his watch, he found out that he had slept in that trance of delirious happiness for a year and eight months.

He suddenly could not breathe and collapsed on the pavement that led to the gate of her heart.

In that same instant, she collapsed into the arms of her childhood friend, shrieking:

"I … I can't breathe," she hyperventilated.

The story of a girl who loved a boy.

The story of a boy who loved a girl.

The story of the man who had entered her soul, leaving the spirit of his ghost to haunt her heart for eternity.

The story of a woman who had caressed his soul into existence, leaving the spirit of her ghost as she carried a deck of pictures—their pictures.

# Take Seventeen

The boy turned the corner.

He ran to play a match of tennis with her.

The boy turned the corner.

He skipped into her arms to watch a movie together.

The boy turned the corner.

He jumped into her reassuring embrace.

The boy turned the corner.

He skydived into the oceans of her heart.

The boy turned the corner.

He smiled and stared up at the girl who lay asleep on the couch.

The boy turned the corner.

He examined her face, as she was engrossed in the comfort of sleep.

The boy turned the corner.

He rushed into the wall that had been built as an obstacle to terminate their love.

The boy turned the corner.

He never doubted his love for her.

The boy turned the corner.

He saw the light of love reflected in her eyes when she looked into his.

The boy turned the corner.

Ashamed that his own family had disrespected their love.

The boy turned the corner.

And saw the crestfallen fragments of her heart surrounding her as she lay on the floor in a heap.

The boy turned the corner.

Once again, against all odds, they had both endured.

The boy turned the corner.

And bid farewell to his heart, not knowing why she had chosen to run away from his.

That boy turned the corner.

Years later, he saw a glimpse of that girl turning another.

That boy turned many corners,

As he followed her silently to her destination.

That boy now stood a meter behind her, about to turn another corner.

He called her name.

That woman turned around—mystified, she stood rooted to the pavement.

Her eyes glowed with the past love of her life.

That man stood in front of her, never wanting to turn another corner without her beside him.

That woman walked gracefully to the boy she once knew and caressed the face of the man she had once loved.

That man and woman hugged tightly, giving birth to the child within them.

There were no more corners to turn.

# Take Eighteen

I was lost.

Lost in the web of possibilities that echoed their existence in my head.

Totally lost, I was abandoned by the passage of time.

Trapped in the certainty that he had cared not, loved not, and dared not phone me again.

Genuinely ill at ease, I pampered myself with life's splendid calamities.

I was lost.

Lost in the labyrinth of no return.

Totally lost in the uncanny play of his character.

Trapped in ways unheard of.

Genuinely astonished, for once upon a time, he was a man of caliber.

I was lost.

Lost in his irony.

Totally lost in his garden of lust and deceit.

Trapped in a dark corner.

Genuinely amused by a man without the voice of reason.

I was lost.

Lost in the reflection of his character.

Totally lost in the absurd behavior of a man with a chronic personality disorder.

Trapped in the light of a smile of intolerance.

Genuinely disappointed with a man who remained indeed no more than a boy.

I was lost.

Lost in the uncertainty that dwelled in his soul.

Totally lost in the river to an ocean of delights.

Trapped in by his selfish tendencies.

Ashamed of my inability to choose a better suitor.

I was lost.

But that was yesterday.

Today I was found in the arms of another man.

A man who took your place.

# Take Nineteen

Insane, I desperately missed your presence in my life.

Insane, I will continue to search for your engine of charms.

Insane, a habit of nostalgia resumed uninterrupted.

Insane, I was left with a fever of love unattended.

Insane, you never heard of a missing heart. It overshadowed your own.

Insane, I left you rooted into the ground, in the dress rehearsal of a groom-to-be.

Insane, I had loved you with an undying passion, with an ecstatic tolerance and a striking compassion sealed with a kiss.

Insane, you loved me completely.

Insane, you completed me, making me whole.

Insane, as we both remain half-empty; our lives now appear, if anything, superficial.

Insane, I smugly delighted your senses, nurturing my own.

Insane, you quenched my thirst for desires unattained.

Insane, and you were insane as well.

Insane, we both stood up in front of the presence of our hearts and lied cruelly about the harbor of our feelings.

Insane, indeed.

Sanity threatened to rebalance my life, ending the essential ingredient of spice that you had delivered to my doorstep almost eleven years ago.

Frankly, I'd rather remain insane.

# Take Twenty

Blind.

Blind without the walking stick, I welcomed the arrival of a man into my life.

My eyes screwed shut; I knew only what the head invented.

The face of the man was in the butt of his personality.

The outline of his body, every curve and high street, was sensed in the radiating warmth of his body up against mine.

His chest was examined by the caressing, gentle hand of a blind lover.

His muscles were flexed in the sensual act of making love.

And this they both did so brilliantly that they made love reappear in the glow of a man's eye and the smooth, compassionate, yet gentle hand of a woman.

Blind, she held on to the key to his door, and without ever seeing the keyhole, she opened the door quickly.

The door swung open in response to her grace.

Inside the room, her eyes settled on her lover as he lay hidden beneath the covers of his sincerity.

Naked, he stood.

He got up and walked over to her.

She saw the outline of his perfectly shaped body and ruffled the curls on his head.

Laughing, he lifted her to a place beyond the constraints of her eyes.

She found herself amid a field of white roses.

She bathed in his sweet scent.

She ate food he had cooked especially for her.

She looked into his eyes and thought of her life before he had trespassed her grounds.

Now she was no longer blind.

Her head rested on his neck.

He had guided her imagination superbly to the extent that the:

Seconds,

Moments,

Hours,

Days,

Months,

And years she spent with him were unlike any other she had known.

Blind she was not.

Not with him.

She walked the path of a blind woman with the help of walking sticks that took the form of a man in love.

He was blindly in love.

She was just in love.

# Sleeping With the Enemy (Part 1)

Today she knew it would happen. Actually, she was waiting for the shit to hit the fan, as the people back home used to say every time a crisis came their way. Lately it seemed like she was always waiting impatiently for the brick to land on her head, the ladder to fall from beneath her, the paint to come scraping off the wall.

Why?

Why was she feeling always at risk?

It was simple. She knew people … almost better than they knew themselves. And those were the nightmares that kept her awake night after night by his side.

And she remained as still as death itself, as if she were in her grave, lying back on the bed with her arms before her and her hands resting on her chest.

# Take Twenty-one

How bizarre?

The world turns around at an unbeatable pace.

People enter your life,

For a season, a reason, or a lifetime.

They smuggle their way into your heart, reaching corners unheard of within.

Stealthily, they absorb your warmest remarks and gather your basketful of kisses.

Of course, neglecting their presence in life's most vulnerable of zones.

Joyfully and welcomed into your borders, they are told about your boundaries and warned not to step over the line of respect.

The men tread softly, tiptoeing around the zone, stopping every now and then to take a nap.

Some of them take short, abrupt naps, while others take comfort in year-long naps.

In their dreams, they find what they have been searching for so desperately in their wakeful days.

Drugged with the arrival of their newfound gifts, they jump up in glee, race to the medicine cabinet, and swallow another handful of sleeping pills.

In a trance, they fall back into the comfort and delicacy of your bed, in the center of the threshold of your heart.

Depending on their neuroses and the number of sleeping pills they swallowed, they fall into dreams of unimaginable proportions.

Asleep for many years, they succumb to lives invented by their imaginations and transformed into reality within their chosen hearts.

There, they learn the beauty of discovering the honey without the painful sting of the bee.

The sweeping arms of time governed by the warmth and hug of a lover.

They melt into her embrace.

Seeking to live a dream.

And that they do.

Until that wet and dreary day when they slowly but gradually wake up from the hypnosis they themselves created. And in sick form they reenter that chaotic world, the same one that promises them times of hardship and deceit.

# Take Twenty-two

She felt like she had just landed the Olympic bronze medal for running the hundred-meter dash. After all, she had won the race against life.

Overwhelmed with a surge of ecstatic happiness, she jumped into the flight and headed back home.

Back to a land that gave birth to the woman of today.

A land that nurtured both her growth and health. Teaching and preaching to her the importance of a solid education.

Today, she ran into the arms of a proud monarchy; yesterday, she would have run into the arms of the most intellectual empire.

Her mum praised her with the warmest sentiment and threw a present into her arms.

The present of a ticket back home.

The ticket that represented a lifestyle only to be found in Europe.

I grew tired of living a lie in a foreign land.

The foreign soil that I casually tiptoed on, with its marvelous weather and oceans of delights scattered among its glamorous skyscrapers and endless sculptures.

Superficiality an asset, it was the most profitable share to buy on the stock market.

I stared, mesmerized by the bundle of shares in my hand.

Without the hindrance of thought, I ditched the shares and watched them fly haphazardly, sinking into the ocean of reality. This may be somebody else's proud and joy.

If truth be told, it was indeed money lost—but after all, there are some things that money can't buy.

And with hope slowly reigniting my bridge of faith, I cried away the last year.

Strange and obscure, I had given up all the money in the world to return to the land of my childhood, my adolescence, and my adulthood.

Arriving at my airport, I inhaled the sweet, suffocating, beautiful scent of a lover by my side.

He stared into my eyes. Tears wavered in his eyes as he signaled the arrival of many more tears into our waterfall.

Turning around, he knelt down and splashed the water, soaking both of us.

We sat drenched in each other's tears as happiness and the love of the past re-conquered the land of our hearts.

# Take Twenty-three

I brushed against the rugged, after-five stubble on his face.

He turned to face me and smiled into my eyes, demanding my pupils to glow in the aftermath of our happiness.

Caressing his face, I blew a kiss on his cheek.

He captured that subtle, delicate kiss and hit a home run.

Pressing his lips against mine, his warmth insulated my shivering, cold-clad body.

Teasingly, he played his lips across the smoothness of my own.

Tracing the line of seduction and maneuvering into second gear, he traced the road of my lips slowly, exciting each nerve.

We were padlocked into a passionate embrace.

I slid my hand down the back of his neck. Coyly, I ran the tips of my fingers along his neck; charming finger-steps met his skin.

Abruptly, he pulled back to reveal a tissue.

A baby pink Kleenex.

Giggling, I playfully pinched his arm.

"I want you to know only one thing now," he whispered.

"I love you," he announced through the delicate microphone of his voice.

Silence.

And it was indeed golden.

A sudden rush of tears headed for the only exit, the corners of my eyes.

Crying—and for the first time, I didn't know why.

Two hot rivers ran down my face like a sauna.

He croaked, "Here, let me wipe away your tears …"

He wiped my tears ever so gently, a lover's hand smoothing the drained rivers of my joy.

He looked at me, his eyes shining like jewels in the light of the full moon.

"I promise to always be there to wipe away all your tears in every season. Here, keep this with you. You may need the tissue later." He briskly held out the tissue for me to hold.

I held the tissue and suddenly realized that it was wrapped around something small and rounded.

Uncovering the baby pink tissue, I found a small box that fit perfectly in my palm.

"Open it," he said.

Opening it, my heart dove straight into the deep end of the ocean.

My eyes met the dazzling sparkle of a diamond ring.

He pulled me closer, bent down on one knee, and asked me to marry him.

I jumped into his arms and kissed him. The shock was slowly but surely absorbed by my surroundings.

A few minutes later, he pulled away, took the tissue from my hand, and explained it all.

"I chose a baby pink, scented tissue, hoping that you would smell it. It's scented with the enchanting smell of roses. Marrying you is promising to make your life—our life—full of the enchanting scent of roses."

Later, we sat on a bench in the park. Under the pitter-patters of raindrops, he told me a truth about life I had never noticed before.

"Always remember today. Remember our love: the way you cried when I told you that I loved you, and how the happiest moment in your life was displayed in the sadness and pain of your tears.

"Life is like that moment.

"In your tears, you welcome the happiest moments of your life.

"One cannot exist without the other."

In that sentence alone, he reminded me why I had loved him.

# Take Twenty-four

I rushed into the arms of a boy who used to swing from tree to tree.

He specialized in sustaining the growth of trees and in his professional swinging techniques.

He swung with a delight, with a thirst for the unknown roots of a tree.

Once he had conquered the joyous world of trees, memorized their growth patterns and been hypnotized with the size of each leaf, he smirked. Laughing at their history, he finally chose to find another profession to master.

He found it in the art of riding horses.

He trained with the appetite of an elephant, galloping on all horses: the blondes, the brunettes, and the black-haired beauties.

Until he had discovered all the varieties of horses, ponies, and much more.

Genuinely aloft, he jumped off the horse one afternoon and realized that he had learned the famous tricks of the trade.

Sleeping under a tree, he awoke to a greater sense of challenge.

One that would prove to be very different from his other conquests.

A boy, not a man, he made a change that would alter his life forever.

He took to the Bank Roads, wandering about endlessly until he found the rate of sex he was expecting.

He found it at the corner of an alley.

He walked into that market and, waving his shares, he demanded his percentage of profit.

Taken aback, the woman delivered a better-than-expected rate of exchange for his bundle of shares.

Smiling with the glee of a boy, he accepted and paid his dues.

They returned later, after the deal was sealed and he had no more shares in his pocket.

Craving much more than his share, he tried desperately searching for that extra share that would land him back at the core of the market.

Unfortunate as he was, he found an unwanted share left to wither away on the side streets of an upper-class area.

He picked her up, thinking with the only mind he exercised.

When they got to a warm and cozy place, he turned and grabbed her, his passion selfishly brimming over onto her. She abruptly withdrew, and before he knew why, a dazzling police badge twinkled at him in the dim light.

In his shock, he couldn't react for a few minutes.

And then, just as easily as that, the tables turned and he was down on his knees, begging for forgiveness and a desperate second chance.

She watched him as he kissed her feet. He didn't want to face such charges in court or, worse yet, a few months in prison.

He pleaded with her.

She timed his pleading and then let him go. Half an hour was more than enough, because he had known that in that half hour alone, she had taught him what other women couldn't teach him: "Always treat others the way you wish to be treated."

Disrespecting him as intended, she walked away. Had she bothered to look back over her shoulder, she would have seen a man left whimpering.

# Take Twenty-five

His eyes lit up with her walking grace as she came to stand beside him.

His best friend longed to find a woman as beautiful and elegant as the one who stood by his friend before the altar.

The sacred flame of their love was united on the grounds of the Christian church.

Her eyes dazzled in response to his look.

Her green emeralds danced around the candle flame of the holy church.

He held her hand, bidding farewell to the life of celibacy and welcoming his vow of commitment to the lady beside him.

They embarked upon the path of life together as one.

They walked back up the aisle, signaling the beginning of an end of celibacy.

Together as man and woman, they welcomed the world with the burning abandonment of two souls.

He crossed the road with hurry in his heel.

He could not wait any longer to embrace the woman he had chosen forever.

She flew into his arms with the might of the wind of love.

He snuggled up against her, and his nose found its long-lost home in the seductive scent that she wore.

Rubbing his nose against hers, he kissed her in all the ways a man could ever kiss a woman.

She smiled into his eyes and toyed with her perfect reflection within them.

A lover she was.

A lover he was.

The same lover they both became.

# Take Twenty-six

He ended their love affair the same way he had begun it all.

Shivering like a leaf, he had grabbed her hand, muttering some delicate prose under his breath, and stopped short under a Chinese tree.

Longingly he had stared into her soul, searching for the right balance of harmony sprinkled with charm and wit.

Fidgeting from foot to foot, he turned his body into a balance.

Then, balancing his whole weight on his right foot, he leaned over and briskly asked her to marry him.

Then, without a further word, he walked away, leaving her dumbfounded.

Years passed, and she bore him a child, fidgety like his dad. He asked a question and never waited for a response.

Another set of years passed by, and the son grew to an adult. He courted a lady without a voice, as she remained quiet most of the time, and proposed to her.

Of course, he was fidgety throughout the proposal.

Although wittier than his dad, the son exercised his inheritance.

He proposed and left, never waiting to hear the response of the lady without a voice.

Weeks passed, months passed, and nothing.

No reply ever came his way.

He retired from the heavy burden she had cast on him and withdrew into a world where he needed no one.

Then one day he went back to the same spot, under that old Chinese tree where he had proposed years earlier, and saw a sight that blinded him for good.

He saw her, six years older, holding a child in her arms.

Aghast, he walked up to her.

Smiling—for there were no more questions to ask the woman who never wanted to marry him.

So without the utterance of any intelligible word or phrase, he took off—*again*.

This time, older and wiser, she ran after him, grabbing him harshly by the back of his shirt and straightening his shoulders in the process.

Angrily, she yelled at him: "You may be able to run away from your lover, but you cannot run away from your son!"

He stopped in his tracks.

Feet glued to the ground, he fell onto his knees and started weeping like a child.

She turned to face him and saw the face of a tired man weeping the sorrows of a special life gone by.

"Why didn't you wait to hear my answer to your proposal?" she asked, gently forgoing her anger and calming down.

He looked up, and in the center of his drowning sorrow, answered: "I thought that in life, you do your part and then leave. Like an actor who says his lines, acts out the scene, and then leaves the stage once his part is over."

"The rest of the story is left up to the other. It's his turn to play out his role, act, and mouth the words that dance around in his heart."

She looked into his eyes and realized at once that there was never a sparkle in them.

He smiled sheepishly, took his son, stared into his delicate features, and blessed him with the certainty that, unlike his own father, he would never let his son down.

A hard lesson, but one that was well learned.

And *think*: all this under the shadows of trees.

# Sleeping With the Enemy (Part 2)

It was the second night with him. It had been as rough as the willow's trunk that peered at her from outside her window. His hands were rugged, and his body just somehow knew the routes into her most erogenous of zones. He even knew his way out of her G-spot, causing her to shiver in delight even as he pulled away from her.

His scent, showered in a condensed version of cologne, drowned her as she tasted his lips. Her force, she once thought, was remarkable, but his passion set new boundaries for her to follow.

She was again lying in bed, thinking of the lusty moments of passion that had been very much a part of her present only an hour ago. She was tired; if she had bothered listening to her body, she would hear it whispering ever so delicately, almost pleading with her to sleep, to give it a rest. But she never knew the meaning or value of rest.

Today was no exception. Her body ached, and her mind was set aflame. He had lit the match and watched as her temperature soared beyond her control and completely under his.

# Take Twenty-seven

She smiled; he laughed.
She sat; he stood.
She smirked; he giggled.
She giggled; he smiled.
He knew happiness; she did not.

She cried; he teared up.
She grew upset; he got annoyed.
She got depressed; he withdrew.
She denied; he applied.
She lived in a well of sorrows; he lived in a well of
        possibilities.
She knew depression; he did not.

She was timid; he was obnoxious.
She was quiet; he was loud.
She was lonely; he was sociable.
She was limited; he was unlimited.
She knew the meaning of being lonely; he did not.

She knelt; he bowed.
She swore; he grew distant.
She denied; he applied.
She withdrew; he retired.
She knew who had been best all along: it was he.
She thought; he did.
She spoke; he realized.
She wished; he received.
She was fending for herself; he was spoiled.
She grew exhausted; he grew energetic.
That's when she knew he was her exact opposite.

*She was the light, and he was its shadow.*

# Take Twenty-eight

He watched, anger erupting in his insides. His eyes, daggers in disguise, promised to cause harm to the woman that stood only a few meters away.

She was oblivious to his daunting presence.

He remained standing, rigid.

She muttered sweet nothings into her lover's ear, laughing joyously in his arms.

He replied with the sweet vengeance of a demanding lover as he graced her lips with a passionate kiss.

Dwelling in each other's arms, they formed their own subjective world where nobody could trespass.

She cuddled him, smothering him in the shadow of her heart.

He watched on as hurt swept over him like a wave slowly but gradually until it hit him, taking his breath away.

His eyes began to march in the protest of the "Pro Waterfall" inquest.

He could not believe his eyes, or why his wife chose to cheat.

They had fallen in love almost a decade ago on that cold winter evening, in that cozy French lounge, in the most famous street in Paris. Champs Elysees, with its grand lifestyle of passers-by, clusters of cafés, and the hidden culture of independent sight.

The human art gallery, as the men watch the women pass by, each with her armored spirit of beliefs; the women watch all the men in their hidden culture and lifestyle as they walk by, and the children leap from store to store, buying the world.

He had first set eyes on her in that lounge as he was courting his coffee to his spot by the sofa, adjacent to the window.

She looked up and smiled, her eyes glowing at the sight of his presence in her chaotic world.

It was then that he suddenly stopped and changed directions, walking over to her table.

Putting his coffee down, he asked her whether sitting and sharing her table would be a good alternative to her solitude.

She had laughed, flipped her hair over to one side, and reminded him that she never owned a table no matter how much she would have wanted to.

And that was when it all began, the love affair of their lives.

It all began with a man sitting down at a woman's table.

The man never left that table again.

Ten years later, his wife, the woman that had spent most of their university years renting that specific table at the French lounge now haphazardly and out of complete character ditched that table and went to rent another, in the arms of another.

His silence was depicted in his misery; his tears, now in full swing, watered the ground beneath him, raining away all their memories. A clean slate appeared in the sunlit path of the morning after. But he was blinded by the glorious rays that penetrated his gaze and caused unnecessary eye pain from squinting.

He turned away, unsure of the consequences he may cause to himself, when his wife just saw him standing there, spying on her new love, as he painfully watched his love evaporate into nothingness.

And so, an hour later, that man walked away from that hindering sight, from his wife and their life forever.

That night, as the woman walked into her apartment, she found it empty, without the presence of a husband in her life, only the presence of his wealth.

She finally cried, drank her last cup of coffee, and waved their love affair good-bye.

# Sleeping With the Enemy (Part 3)

His name was as difficult as he was to figure out. Shlovenski was a man that was used to many women following him, oohing and aahing around him. They scattered around him daily, giving him reason to believe that he was indeed the best lover in the world. After all, that was the only thing he knew how to do in life, and the only thing that came naturally to him. Sometimes being around people reminded him of his many hidden insecurities and his main incapability to maintain a job or even to be passionate about a career.

But that never saddened him. He never felt the need to go beyond the call of duty—actually, if truth be told, he was just content with everything in his life as it was in the present. He had no ambitions, no aching questions that were left unanswered, and to him his destiny was obvious: he was devoted to his chosen religion, which many believed could be interpreted to say that destiny was predetermined for him in God's great plan. So why should he go against that grain of thought? Shouldn't he, as a part of that faith, be thankful for his life and what God chose to bestow on him? Who was he to interfere in God's plan?

And that's why he spent his many days at a job that was only guaranteed and presented to him on a silver platter due to being born into a particular family. He never really learned the beauty of self-creating something that was so out of his reach, the marvel at choosing the right goal to aim for and score. Instead he was taught that what bestowed upon him all the innocent pearls was the wisdom to be able to access that which was laid out in front of him at birth. A shocking fact to many but not to him.

To him, some things were a blessing that could not go ignored. But what intrigued me the most was his incapability to notice that he was indeed his own worst enemy. After all, he hid behind his magical cloak 355 days a year, with the remaining days in complete exposure.

But in this cloud, there was a slim, silver lining. He had one talent: in the first ten minutes you spoke to him, he charmed you. And really, in retrospect that's all he had.

Why I was involved with him was completely beyond my understanding. Why was I so attracted to this man that to me resembled the broken columns of failure? Could it be that opposites attracted that much?

Lately I have been shocking myself into decisions that were, if anything, out of my character.

# Take Twenty-nine

I ran into the arms of my lover.

He was dressed in the mentality of an intellectual, was wrapped up warmly in the inquiries of religion, and wore philosophical gloves at hand.

He was tall, lean, and dependable, just like the Eiffel Tower.

Many women of all ages enjoyed a climb up his tower of elegance, as he marveled at showing them views, scenery of the city of all hearts.

They clustered around him like pigeons groveling for their last piece of bread. He watched them eating away, hungering after his bread, while other birds just grew impatient with his morsels of food.

A whole breed of them flew away, set their wings in motion, and leapt off the mountain of compassion and love. Leaving the most wanted man alone. Although only for a short time, until his harbor was conquered again with the birds of the special colored feathers. Experience was engraved into the plaque of his soul.

He had traveled the tunnel of all experiences in the whim of his early twenties. He spent a decade drowning in his love waters, learning what moved them, what excited them, what boiled them into an uncontrollable frenzy, and finally what waves he needed the most.

Now at thirty-five years of age, he smiled in the light of all his vast collection of antique love affairs, laughed in the showers of his past hurt, and cried in the solitude of his existence.

A woman rescued him from his lonely waters. She dove into his turbulent dark waters, rescued him from beneath the most ironic cold and thrashing waters. Carrying him, she laid him on the sandy shore, wiped away his tears, dried up his shriveled body, and aligned his body with the intense heat and brightness of the sun. Breathing into his mouth, she calmed his nerves and taught him that the art of meditation, as enriching in mind as in body, was indeed a spiritual awakening to life's purpose.

He lay beneath her gaze, mesmerized in her beauty.

But most of all he was hypnotized with her charm that lay intricately hidden in the beads of her personality.

That woman, he thought, as his eyes hovered over her body while she lay asleep in his bed next to him, dreaming of yet another rescue.

That woman was now his.

# Take Thirty

Entering the borders of a new world, I entered.

Entering the borders of professional dancing, I entered.

Entering the class of lambada, I entered.

Entering the seductive rhythm of dance, I entered.

Entering the arms of men dancing with me, I entered.

Entering the arms of that man full of sexual enticement, I entered.

Entering the sweet sweat of a dancing performance unlike any other, I entered.

Entering the flavor of seduction at the heel, I entered.

Entering from the withdrawal of a seasonless world, I entered.

Entering the arms of my soul, I escaped.

Entering your arms was a dangerous endeavor for your soul, bowed to my own, making love on the dance floor.

I broke away from the borders of dance, of the enticing trance of a world, returning to my seasonless but safe world.

What a pity…

# Take Thirty-one

I awoke in the morning and sat up in my bed.

Crouching, I scratched my head.

I turned and faced the window of possibilities.

Staring into the beauty of London, overshadowed in the cloudiness of a land burdened with intellectual debates that took residence in its soil.

I cried a tear, a tear of happiness.

Happiness echoed in the glow of my eyes.

Even at 7:30 in the morning, my skin glowed in the freshness of the bitter cold, piercing wind of my land.

I turned and faced him again.

He was still asleep.

Dispersed in the heat of the moment, I caressed his face, awakening him to a gentle kiss.

His eyes wide open, he turned and shielded my body with his.

Above me, he controlled the foreplay of seductive kisses that inhabited our lips.

Fighting a duel of kisses, we rolled around in bed, swapping control, and fell onto the hardness of our marble floor.

Laughing, we scrambled to our feet and rushed racing to the bathtub.

He filled the tub with the gushing hot water of our passion, and I searched for our collection of candles.

Finding them, I spent the next half hour creating the sanctuary of our love in the boundaries of our bathroom.

I placed vases around the sink, giving birth to a river among endless rivers of candles lit with the alluring scent of lovers at bay.

I sprinkled a rose fertilizer on the marble floor.

Red rose petals haunted the floor of our bathroom.

I placed a silver statue of Peace at the corner of the left side of the sink, behind the large vase with the red, round candles that swam in the water when the breeze gently pushed them along.

The bathtub was now refilled with waters of my soul. Throwing in half the bubble bath formula along with a handful of white rose petals, I laughed.

They swam reluctantly in the hot waters, dressing the water with the brightness of their white petals and shreds of hope.

Unexpectedly, a scream escaped the opening slant of the bathroom door.

It echoed its surprise, ringing a bell of fear in my ears.

Running out of the bathroom, I almost tripped on the bunch of nails that had gathered over time at the corner of the entrance to the bathroom.

In anguish, I ran to the window of our bedroom and found my lover huffing and puffing with his hand caught in the trap of the window.

Frantically he tried yanking his fingers out of the grip of the windowsill, but could not.

On an impulse, I heaved up the window, holding the weight of it upon my thin, unstable arms, and yelled at him to yank his hand out.

Half an hour later, we were in the kitchen tending to his bruised hand with the help of the first aid kit.

That night, both asleep in the warmth and coziness of our bed, we took a journey along the valley of our dreams.

I awoke to find my lover absent from my bed.

After that, every day I awoke in the solitude of his absence.

# Take Thirty-two

I lay scattered among the histories and memories of a time gone by.

The papers, bright at one stage in their life, now have turned obscurely beige at each corner.

Beige with the growth of time and vast number of years, even decades, gone by.

I picked up one snapshot of a past memory.

A smiling face full of happiness greeted me.

My face was alive with the warmth and compassion of my lover as he stood behind me, hugging me away from the harshness of reality.

His bare arms were exposed, and his fruitful grin saluted my smile.

His grin, after all, lived in the shadow of my smile.

His eyes, little brown jewels, appeared red in the picture.

He was indeed a ruby among a wave of non-precious stones.

We were both really cold, standing in front of our favorite night club.

We paused a fraction of a second that night before running into the club to dance the night away in each other's arms, sailing into each other's dreams as the night grew old, giving way to the birth of another new day.

Closing my eyes momentarily, I watched the night reappear before my very eyes.

That rainy, cold, bitter, and foggy day in January 2000.

That Friday, all the Fridays of a lover's past.

A night when we reunited to celebrate our youth, satisfy our thirst for cocktails, and most importantly of all, share endless songs and dancing.

"Yes," I giggled now, caught in the movie of my past flame on that eventful evening.

We ran like mice on a pedestal up the stairs of the club to reach the bar and dance floor area.

He hugged me with all his might. I was hugging the man who had seductively and intelligently captured my cheeky happiness and then gifted me with it.

The man who made my days worth more than their weight in gold, made my hours powerful with the ecstasy of his existence, and made my minutes all moments to be treasured.

He reminded me of the intensity of seconds as he lay naked in my arms.

We shivered into a night of endless encounters as we rolled around, wrestling away our passion.

His body a blanket that insulated further heat within, a blanket that wrapped around the corners of my body, protecting me against the bitter cold sting of solitude.

But that was all just in his hug.

His hug was the preview to the movie of PPS: "Possible Passionate Struggles."

And as we parted, I kissed his cheek lightly, welcoming the breeze of seduction in my wake.

He turned and kissed me, scattering all his kisses around my face, like a fertilizer carefully planting the seed of possibilities.

And then we jumped up abruptly and ran to the dance floor to dance to the rhythm of our bands.

And we danced, danced like there was no tomorrow, nor yesterday.

We were living, breathing, and dancing away the minutes of our present.

Little had I known then that he was giving me the present of the moment, guided lustfully by irreplaceable memories.

Hours later, after we had worn out the soles of our feet and the swaying rhythm of our waists, we retired into the freezing early morning night.

And despite all efforts from friends to drive both of us home, we stubbornly welcomed the music of our shoes dancing to the subtle beat of our walk all the way back to my home.

We walked arm in arm, forming a chain of strength built from the harmony of our love.

We talked about the whole world that early morning, smiling, grinning, laughing, giggling, and ended the night with the rain of a bitter cold winter day.

It rained on us as he stood by my house, hugging me and whispering words.

My eyes stung and I rained, crying and receiving the sweetest, most fragile words from the lips of my lover.

"I love you."

He stared in disbelief at my tears, and without warning glared at me and started his own raining episode.

I immediately wiped his tears with my fingers, kissing the trails of his tears as they stained his face.

We hugged each other and continued hugging each other, whispering our secrets into the other's keeping.

I don't know how long we stayed that night hugging, but when we finally parted, it was 6:00 AM, and we had exited the club a long while ago.

We must have spent twenty minutes walking to my place and the rest locked in each other's embrace.

A tear ran along my face now, as an adult.

I never again encountered that same voyage of love.

Not in the same way.

And as I looked at the snapshot, words lost all their meanings.

I smiled, grinned, laughed, and giggled ...

And cried.

I worried that he may have found comfort in renting out his heart to another's keeping.

And since I was not there to keep it, I stood in the solitude of a hug never to return.

A snapshot, a memoir ...

# Sleeping With the Enemy (Part 4)

He was waiting today for me, in his place, as is always the case. I drove to his house and just stood outside in the warm heat of the night. I did not enter.

I don't know why I came, but I was glued to the front of his door, unable to take a step forward or even a step back to my car in the garage.

And I must have stood there for almost an hour toying with my decision: to be or not to be?

Should I go inside and greet him as I always do, with a kiss on his cheek, and then make passionate, shameless love to him over and over again? To a man I can neither comprehend nor respect?

Is that what I really thought of myself? Did I value myself so little that I chose an uneducated, illiterate man? Who in their right mind would want that for themselves?

I was never like this—never hesitant and never that destructive. But his touch, his feel, held my mind in captivation. The logic housed there stood no chance against such an overpowering surge of physical chemistry.

And so I finally relented and went in with my head hanging low. This was wrong, and I knew it.

# Take Thirty-three

He walked along the bar, moving along the multitude of people.

I entered the bar, immediately searching for the man I knew only too well.

And I caught his handsome face in the reflection of the lamp on the side of the bar.

The reflection of a man with soft hair that fell seductively over the suburbs of his face, eyes that bore the soul of a genuinely deep, loving person, and lips that shone and dimmed, playing a game of hide-and-seek with women of all ages.

It wasn't until I stood in front of him that I realized that his magnetic pull extended right into my reach. It had pulled me across the dance floor and lured me into a corner that was draped with velvet curtains.

Standing in front of him, I smiled and waited for him to make a move. A couple of minutes later, that's exactly what he did.

Kissing me on my cheek, he pulled me in for a wholesome hug. We became an artwork of two bodies lurking in each other's keeping.

Between crowds of people, two souls had ignited in the consuming flame of their past.

The whole world, groups of people smothered in the intensity of their dancing, the heat and rebirth of a bar, and the all time humidity as each man and woman danced against the dance floor, listening to the rhythm of their hearts.

That whole fiasco just melted into nothingness.

Reaching for my hand, he led me to the dance floor.

He danced rather slowly.

I fell into the well of rhythm, floating to a destination that only two people inhabited.

The man who sparked my soul into a flame and the woman who ignited at his touch.

Dancing, laughing, we emerged alone but together as one.

Up against his body, he mapped out my own, fitting into my curves.

Reading my expression, he knew. He could see the words that lit up on the outskirts of my face as they tiptoed in unity with the disco lights.

Throwing back my head in laughter, I said, "I guess I'm the keyhole and you're the key."

And today I am reminded of the time that we danced to a ballad of sexual fervor that did little to ease the pain of losing one another. Years later, we will continue where we left off—that is, if destiny permits.

# Take Thirty-four

He brushed his hand against my knee.

A gentle wave of emotions flushed my fears away.

He had touched me. Again.

A relief dug a hole in the past well of sorrows.

A shiver escaped my body as the coldness found its residence in the hollow emptiness of my bones.

On an impulse, he wrapped his arms around me, enclosing me in his world.

A smile dared to break out on my face.

I smiled like never before.

Not for over five years, anyway.

My lips seemed to find joy in this beautiful stretching exercise.

Growing lazy over the years, they had outgrown an exciting, energetic lifestyle.

Previously craving a bite of the healthy gym workout, they somehow failed to find their perfect match.

And now, giggling, I finally smiled my way out of my past depression, leaving behind in my wake a paranoid, frantic girl.

He caressed my face gently, his rough hand in friction with my baby-soft skin.

I closed my eyes only briefly and responded to his heightened sense of touch.

I fell into a trance, a trance guided by his wonderful, brisk fingers.

He cupped my face in his hands reassuringly and whispered, "Open your eyes."

Slowly, I opened my eyes and saw him.

He was crying.

His eyes shining in the shadow of his tears, tear after tear.

My eyes watered as I cried silently.

Crying for the love that we had both buried. We had attended its funeral and then mourned its absence.

It must have been the most intense two hours I had ever spent.

I wore bright colors in the hope of hiding the pitiful sorrows of a love that I had so easily ditched, thus masking my greater depression.

He was surprisingly wrapped in the armor of a man in mourning.

Black, but ironically, black suited him most.

That was him: a man of considerable virtues, a man of wealth.

His wealth was indescribable, for it was the wealth of a well-acclaimed personality.

He was the richest man in the world, ranked first in *Fortune* and in my personally tailored *Forbes* edition.

I leaned over and licked the path of his tears with my tongue.

Pausing and regaining my composure, I moved to the left cheek and continued assaulting the trail of tears with the weapon of my tongue.

He suddenly withdrew and, blinking at me, he intensified the moment. Holding both of my hands together, he kissed them and put them in his lap.

I had stopped crying.

"Why?" I cracked, as my voice choked up with feelings for him.

He stood up. Grabbing my hand, he walked me out with him.

Outside the bar, he inhaled deeply and turned to face me.

For a few seconds we stood just inches apart, teasing our sexual appetite into obedience.

He pulled me toward him and drew my face close.

He kissed my lips, teasing the surface of my lips with the soothing surface of his own.

He leaned over to my ear, and that's when and how our past flame was rekindled.

# Take Thirty-five

He walked into the flat.

A man of the past in the glamour and pride of the present.

A smile greeted me with the mischievous character lurking beneath his face.

I opened the door to our past.

Surprisingly, this door was the most natural of all to open.

A strong, refreshing draft wafted in, freeing my hair to dance in the rhythm of the moment.

I inhaled the scent of young, blooming roses in the most enchanting bouquet. A ribbon of noncommitment shielded the roses from reality.

I blinked in the doorway. Visions of our heated seconds, moments of passion, slid right in front of my eyes, the audience of my soul.

Glowing with memories fueling my blood, I laughed, welcoming him back into the present.

He walked back into my life, flying in from the destination known as the "the past half a decade" region.

Landing at the front step of my door, he arrived to the "matured lover's" region.

He pulled a ticket from his pocket and threw it at me with the glimmer of suspense and seduction in his eyes.

I abruptly grasped the ticket in my palm, stopping its journey in midair.

Opening my palm, my eyes watered over the words that were immediately absorbed in the sponge of my heart.

"Destiny is in seeing what you have always wanted and leaving it at that."

Looking at the crumpled ticket in my palm, I knew the absurdity of our encounter. It was written in very small print on the back of the ticket.

I looked at him, a man exquisitely dressed in dark brown, elegance his virtue, smoldering good looks and a radiating charm illuminating the path in front of him.

I threw the ticket away—after all, it was a used one—and turned to face him.

He spread the sexiest smile on his lips and echoed the words of a humorous man.

Chattering away, many moments were filled with our noisy, spontaneous remarks.

Remarks and conversations ran along the highway of the same mind.

How does the saying go? "Great minds think alike." And this was no exception.

Words encrypted the wall of the living room, designing our room and at once inviting the succession of easiness into our lives.

We rocketed on now, on the couch, with the shadow of a background movie.

Throwing pebbles of punctuation at one another, a conversation of gentle, smooth, yet dynamic interaction.

And that's when it all happened.

He grabbed the champagne bottle and with one swift move and popped the cork of passion back into our lives.

Laughing, I grabbed my hands and tried to stop the sudden leaking of the champagne around the body of the bottle.

His hands met mine, and a giggle escaped the sarcastic corners of my heart.

A surge of warmth and heat spilled over my hands. Feeling his hands radiate my fingers, I immediately shied away and pulled them back.

He went after them and, caressing my hand, massaged the champagne cream into my skin.

Bending down, he licked my right hand clean of the sparkling champagne droplets.

He drank with the art of licking.

Subdued, I remained as solid as a brick, never even budging an inch.

My eyes were busy witnessing the outbreak of the sense of touch.

Inhaling the heat of candles drenched in the aroma of cinnamon, my imagination went into overdrive.

He peered up at me and let his eyelids communicate the outbreak of a moment long overdue.

I pulled his face up to my level and, looking into his eyes, I saw the flourishing of a love, the shining hope of a life about to begin, all fixated in the sexual enlightenment of a man looking at his woman.

Closing my eyes, my head guided my passion to his lips.

I gently licked his lips, pecking them into action.

A sudden surge of heat collided in our bodies, sending me flying into the labyrinth of his mouth as we both toyed with our boundaries and experimented with all corners: obvious, hidden, and shielded ones.

All at once we were locked into a passionate embrace, catching up on the last four years of absence.

He pulled me onto his lap, seating me in the center of him.

He took my right arm and, pulling up my sleeve, he planted warm kisses all along the suburbs of my arm. Almost immediately, I stopped him abruptly and began kissing his neck, teasing the bass of sexuality in his earlobe.

My tongue taught him the sound of a language known only to lovers.

He ran his fingers through my hair strand by strand and tilted my head to one side.

He gently attacked my smooth neck with the warmth of his tongue, gently sweeping away the essence of my perfume. His tongue danced in the rhythm of seduction, twirling around the edge of my ear.

His hands found the barrier of clothing in our encounter.

He grabbed my tight-fitting blouse and massaged it off my bare body.

Recognizing the activity, my bra signaled to him.

He pulled back and stared at me.

His eyes memorized every inch of my neck and my round, fruitful breasts hidden beyond the bra.

Unexpectedly, he grabbed me and pulled me.

He ran his tongue from my neck all the way down the center to the bottom of my stomach.

His tongue, a masqueraded feather, tantalized with shivers of delight.

He held me in his arms and rocked me back and forth, gently swinging me onto the couch next to him.

He stood up, towering above me.

He performed the beginning of a teasing strip show as he slowly unbuttoned his jeans, allowing his trousers to drop casually at his feet.

He smiled, a horny man with the largest smile plastered on his lips, as he moved back a meter away from me.

Facing me with just his white boxers, he said, "Look at me. I'm your man." He whispered gently, as if almost afraid that someone else would hear him.

I got up slowly and walked over to him; all the while, my eyes were glued to his.

He grabbed me and slowly unzipped my trousers, throwing them aside.

Slowly, he smoothed my body in the palms of his hands, bent down, and unwrapped my G-string.

Drinking the river of expectation, he sent me to a land beyond dreams.

Minutes later, he grabbed me and swung me to the wall, crucifying me on the wall of my room for the very first time.

A gentle lover, he was.

Playing my body, molding it into a sculpture of passion, and massaging my aches and pains with his supportive, delicate strength, he made love to me.

A composer he was, as he strung his body into mine, composing a new melody of desire and vibrating spontaneity.

The music was gentle, smooth, and created a hunger for a new melody that only our two bodies could create.

Later, as I lay crumpled in the arms of my man, I delicately wove a love of no boundaries in my heart.

We lay hovering in and out of sleep, on the floor, covered in a duvet.

I fell asleep in a trance of harmony.

Peaceful harmony. I celebrated my love in his arms.

I awoke to the dreary cold early morning, turned over, and found beside me my man, holding the crown of a woman.

He kissed me gently and crowned me finally, a woman in every sense.

My innocence and childish demeanor still haunt the walls of that room.

I winked at the man in front of me, but in reality I winked at the child that was no longer a part of me.

# Sleeping With the Enemy (Part 5)

He stared at me as I walked right in through the door. I just walked up to him and kissed him. I unbuttoned his trousers and slowly stripped him, not only of his clothes but of his dignity as well.

I did not stop—I could not stop—nor could I pull back from his poisonous embrace for a breath of much-needed air.

I was like a demon, possessed enough to work myself and him into a destructive frenzy. I warmed at his touch as his tongue played a silent duel with mine.

My body was aroused—so aroused that my underwear signaled the beginning of my arousal.

It was too late now to change all that had happened, and too late to change what was happening now. All I kept thinking was that it was too late for it all—it was too late for everything to go back to normal.

It was too late. And as impatient as I was, I hated to be confronted with the ugly truth, but this time I had no choice. I either got busy living or dying in a spiral of no return. The stakes remained high, but then again it was part of my character and nature to risk things to get what I have always dreamed of.

It's not true what people tell you. You never stand a chance of changing; that's why you just change situations, context, and the environment around you. Adults who tell you that they can change a part of themselves are just lying. And people are actually prone to be liars; they actually have a dominant gene that releases chemical feel-good endorphins every time they lie.

I should know, because I was the biggest liar of my time.

# Take Thirty-six

I danced in the arms of a man of speed.

Envisioning my odd reality, I embarked on a journey of pace.

Wrapping my arms around his neck and playing with his curls, I danced in circles around the man who had no heart but rhythm.

His movements were scattered around the dance floor for me to follow. But I was not a follower and never will be.

He danced now, apart from me, creating a painting of foot strokes and fast glides. He paused, waiting for me to respond, but I never did. Watching from afar proved far more worthy of my time.

He ran across the dance floor and whipped his body in a circular motion in midair before landing right by my feet.

And still no reaction.

He dragged another woman from the whirlpool of dancers that surrounded him. It was, I had to admit, superb dancing in duos. But that still did not evoke much of a reaction from me.

Finally, his hands shot up in the air in surrender, and I could almost feel the breeze of goose bumps of the white flag tickle my arms and legs. But even that did not capture enough of my interest.

As I was busy enjoying the many tastes that worldly wines had on offer, he walked over and interrupted my drinking from the well of knowledge.

"I don't get it. All other women are impressed with my professional dancing. Why should you be the only exception?" he asked, totally gobsmacked.

"A dance is enriched with passion, right?"

"Of course."

"Well then, what's the use of dancing with one without the passion of a heart?"

Turning and finally facing him, I saw it. He not only descended in my eyes, but his too.

The woman who changed a man through changing how he saw himself. Difficult to do, I know, but definitely not impossible.

# Take Thirty-seven

A lover I am.
A child I was.
A woman I had become.

A man.
A stranger of lust.
A lover he had become.

A lover, a child, and a man.
He had it all.
The different colors of life.
The shadows of violence and sincerity.
The light of passion and the cloud of despair.

His genuine character.
His forbidding grace.
His unfortunate paranoia.
His delights, all hand-carved into sculptures of beauty.

He was a man of wonder.
A man of creations.
He invented a woman, his woman.
She casually welcomed his delusion in life.
She dwelled at his touch.
Aching for his being and never retiring from his love.
She loved him in ways no one understood.
She taught him her definition of love.
The pleasure of sacred sharing and the rejoicing of life in
       twos.

He learned.
Learned the lesson of love.
How to love unselfishly.
How to deny himself virtues.
He lived in a world she managed.
Until that day that he smirked in the eyes of celibacy.

He moved into the permanent residence of her soul.
Promising never to return.

She lived on a mountain.
Above the average horizon,
With her dreams,
And she successfully lived out her own.
Her own dream,
Now forever theirs.

# Take Thirty-eight

I was swept away.
Far away,
Into the wholesome feeling of completeness.
You completed me, giving life to the missing half of my
        heart.
Shielded by your own arteries, it felt alive.
Alive, with each exhilarating breath.
Functioning as a whole, it gave rise to your unbeatable
        zeal.
Never at risk of heart failure, you tailored it carefully,
        massaging it elegantly.

I inhaled a deep, excruciating breath of cold fresh air,
Exhaling it from your lungs,
Shivering in ecstasy in your arms, I lay among the
        warmth of my own.
Hugging you into my life, I smothered myself.

Walking down the path of life,
I heard footsteps,
A gentle tiptoeing of shoes,
Click-clack, click-clack,
I walked on faster,
Click, click, click …
Stopping abruptly,
I could no longer hear the tiptoeing of my shoes,
Looking ahead of me,
There you were,
Walking in front of me,
But without the sound of your feet christening the
      ground.
Perplexed, I stood.
Then ….
Taking a step or two,
I heard the click-clacking sound of our feet walking the
      same path.
That's when the realization hit me,
If we walk together,
We make one sound.
Walking alone,
We make no sound.
*As you are a part of me,*
*And I will always remain a part of you.*

# Sleeping With the Enemy (Part 6)

He carefully cupped my right breast in his hand and massaged it delicately between his palm and fingers. He let loose the other to preach its hardening existence silently to the wind.

His hands molded me into his finest creation: a woman aching to feel him within her. I became the sculpture he had vowed he would make of me that first day he had set his eyes on me back in the fall.

My body quivered with delight as he slowly but surely caressed my left thigh under my skirt. His fingers mapped the path to my G-spot, and he had me almost crying for his touch.

He briskly teased me into submission with a rhythm that spoke volumes to my body and one that understood the language of my body's most vulnerable need.

I was whisked away into seconds of delight, mountains fresh with dew, roses of the most passionate grace, and rain that showered the doubts into oblivion.

I was his, and for a few seconds more he would remain mine. All I needed was the ecstatic volcano that sent my body shivering in its wet aftermath.

After that, all that was left was calmness and peace. I had not known the feeling of peace or its most damning presence until he had pushed my boundaries to welcome it into my world. From now on, peace was, to me, his touch in my body.

# Take Thirty-nine

He stood under the threshold of our school,
Holding up the wall with his continuous persistence.
He prevailed beyond my wildest imaginations.
A man—perhaps a boy, trapped in the body of a
    stubborn, relentless man.

He smiled at the kids playing in the schoolyard.
Dismissing his child of wonder, he stood.
A phase of maturity clouded his mind,
Dwelling in the house and land of tomorrow.
He forgot to outlive the pearls of innocence of a child at
    play.

An adult in a child's body, he exhausted his body.
Discarding it,
Forcing the man within him to live on.
And what of the child at play, innocence etched in his
    features, dreams embodied in his soul? Tears
    knew not his territory.

That same child turned and stared at the man holding up
    that column.
He stared intensely into his eyes,
Never letting down his penetrating, challenging gaze.
He found no happiness, a trademark lost to the man in
    front of him.
He found in its place,
A responsible, daunting look woven in wrinkles around
    the eyes of that man.
He ran to him,
And fell into his arms,
Hugging him beyond comprehension.
And just as quickly withdrew,
Back into the playground,
Into his territory of story-telling, toys, cupcakes, and
    hide-and-seek.
He hid from that man,
And begged to understand why the man never knew the
    art of living.

Running back at the end of break time,
He opened the man's hand and placed a treasure there.
It was a sticker from a collection of his favorite G.I. Joe
    albums.
"I know how important it is to collect stickers,
"And it's time for you to realize that you should treasure
    the stickers of moments in life in your album.
"Pictures you never ever stop collecting, even at your
    age," he told him.

And with the giggle of a child at play,
He withdrew, never to return.
The man cried silently,
A child he had once known,
Played in the memories of his youth.

And that is how,
That man found the child within him.

# Take Forty

He looked at me. His eyes wove the blanket of the secret of our love.

A sunbeam threatened to overwhelm my being as I glanced in his direction.

His voice was the sweetest melody, in tune with my own.

Charmed, I stood inches away from my lover.

His eyes remained remarkably genuine and gentle.

He delicately removed a strand of hair from my face and continued to stare imploringly at me.

I could feel the tornado of happiness hold my heart in its grasp.

It was a moment unlike any other.

A moment I least expected.

He was the wind beneath my wings.

The gentle breeze that tickled my skin awake in the early morning sun.

Gasping for air, I froze.

I had grown reluctant over the years with the men in my life.

Learning never to expect much from them.

But now, as I stood frigid with shock, I realized that he was the only exception.

He had always been the only exception.

It was a far greater virtue to love the man of your dreams.

And as a tear watered my cheek, I knew that *that* man was the one for me.

# Take Forty-one

She looked at me, and her eyes spoke the words I had been dreading.

Sneering, she welcomed me back into the world governed by superficiality.

I stared at the people walking in and out of shops, people of all shapes and sizes, making up the walk of life as I know it.

Only they were not really part of that walk.

The whole world carved and craved a living of substance; these predators lived in a glamorous shell of artificial endurance.

Ironically, they have grown up living a lie.

I shrugged my shoulders and started fidgeting with the set of keys in my pocket.

The keys that bred my existence into the land of idiocy.

"What a deceitful living," I muttered under my breath.

A betrayal to reality if there ever was one.

The faces were ghostly, expressionless as they slowly walked past me; I cried silently at the corner of the mall, adjacent to the ladies' bathroom.

Crying away my past, even my future, as I found myself stuck in the mud of the present.

Almost at once, the flood of despair possessed my being.

I was forced to decline the offer of my home to come to this uncanny display of a missing world. A Legoland that transgressed humane boundaries.

Unexpectedly, I found myself staring insignificantly at the ceiling above me.

An astonishing display of architecture swiveled around the center of my pupils.

Their designs were elaborate, perfectly flown in from the cultural capital of the world, Rome. This much was apparent.

I suddenly bit into my finger, struggling to keep my rising anger at bay.

I closed my eyes and envisioned a flight back home.

Upon arrival, I felt the rush of insulating warmth circulate through my whole body like my blood supply.

The intense brightness of the sun showered an electric trance of hope.

"This is what it's got to feel like, when I'm part of my future," I thought, glancing momentarily at the environment that surrounded me as it slowly but surely came to a stop in front of my eyes.

I was finally in the powerful shadow of the brightest of suns.

Funny that I never knew that paradox—crying tears of delight.

Until this instant.

And rejoicing in the splendor of the moment, I cried away all my tears, swallowing them down with gulps of happiness.

Walking the roads of my childhood, I relived the ecstasy of a life gone by.

Walking elegantly on the pavement, I stumbled on a few pebbles, the pebbles of memories long gone.

Kneeling down momentarily on the road, I carefully assembled the remaining pebbles.

My back, now a radiator, met the sun in its full glow as it set in the distance.

Out of the blue, a man appeared in front of me. He pulled my hand into his and, opening my palm, took a pebble and held it up to the night sky.

In his tender touch, his thrilling stroke, my heart fluttered.

It was him.

The man who had cheekily preoccupied the days of my youth.

Holding up my chin, my gaze soon followed.

I looked into his eyes, silently.

Although he was speaking, I could not hear his voice; instead I read the script that he delicately strung together for me.

Reading his eyes, it became all too apparent.

His eyes tearfully retold my story, leading me into another of my own making.

And at night, in the dim light of my lamp beside my bed, that was the story that I began creating. The rest? Well, you will just have to read it.

Words of the past; books of a future.

# Sleeping With the Enemy (Part 7)

"I want you! I need you, goddamn it!" he said, his voice screeching to be heard. "Why don't you understand? Why?"

He was getting desperate now.

"Are you bloody doing this on purpose? Are you? Is this payback time? Well, is it?"

I finally had him where I wanted. My wish had been answered.

"Stop screaming and calm down. You know very well that this is not about you or us; it's about principles and ethics in life," I said icily.

"No. You know that's bullshit."

I could almost feel his anger fueling the blood in his veins. He had to learn and, unfortunately, I was the one who was going to teach him.

I grabbed his arm and stopped him from leaving the room. "Stop now. This is beginning to get out of hand—just stop."

He turned to face me. His face was as red-hot and bothered as the peppers that were my favorite ingredient in my pasta sauce. Just as I chopped my vegetables and sliced my peppers for my sauce, I also made sure that I mixed the sauce and let it simmer slowly but gradually on the stove until it boiled.

I would do the same with him. He was as spicy as the chili, and just as dangerous. And I was about to test my control over him.

What's the worst that could happen? And just as the thought was released, so was the fear that gripped me.

Be careful what you wish for. And I had forgotten to be careful—yet again.

# Take Forty-two

I was walking through Christopher's Place, skipping in and out of beats to the dance that drummed its rhythm, echoing in my ears.

Entering the first bar on my left, I wafted into the bar, floating into the whimsical choreography of bodies.

As I sat down, I found myself right below an abstract painting in the art gallery section of the bar.

The painting appeared to resemble a work of sexual art stuck in the ambiguous sight of the gazer.

The artist had painted a man's chest smack in the center of the painting, a nude upper body of a man in the middle of a whirl of colliding colors.

"How remarkable," I said out loud to no one in particular as I studied the painting.

His naked body hung in the center of the painting, almost as if he was hanging on by a thread, waiting for his other half, in nude form, to come to his rescue.

I chuckled, thinking of the vulnerability of that man, at wit's end and waiting for the reassuring arms of his woman. The woman who would not only rescue him but re-balance his state of mind.

Taking another sip of my cocktail, I dove into the painting above me in a voyage of discovery, determined to unravel the identity of the man who appeared so sensual in nature.

Holding the paintbrush in hand, I started painting and sketching his upper body into my reality.

With every stroke of my brush he shivered, goose-bumping within an inch of reality.

By the time I had sketched his belly button I stood back, very pleased with myself as I noticed that I had now a half-naked man, fidgeting and squirming, anxiously moving around and trying to discover his painter.

*Me.*

As I reached the moment of drawing his trousers and buttons, I abruptly decided to dump my paintbrush into the waste bin and walk away from the painting.

From a distance, I looked up at him and found a nude, faceless man. I was overwhelmed with the daunting feeling of vulnerability that sent my body shivering into semi-spasms.

Opening my eyes slowly, I kissed his belly button, smoothing the way with my tongue.

Working my way up, I drew to a halt, admiring the extravagant display of a six-pack.

With a dangerous smile, I peered closer at him, at once seduced. I had to learn, study every inch of this man. The muscles that gave way to the grounded and toned six-pack at his core.

Slowly but surely I had done it again. I painted the nude man with my own version of an erotic paintbrush: that of my tongue.

I dwelled in the most sensitive of regions on his neck.

An impressionist I became as I pecked his neck into color.

Warming his neck with the heat of my own, I reached the end of it, looked up, and for the very first time saw the face of my invisible man.

He somehow occupied the face of the man who had christened me for the very first time.

Hugging me, he reminded me that sometimes things are not what they seem, and that was their beauty.

Hugging him back, hard, I fell into a spinning whirl of musical colors surrounding his body and now surrounding my own.

Colors inhabited both our souls as we swam together in the ocean of fantasy.

We now live in the presence of a life bombarded by ecstasy and color, neglecting the neutral glow of celibacy.

This has become our only reality.

# Take Forty-three

I swam away. My high-flying strokes sliced through the crispy cold waters of the pool with the ease of gliding speed.

Swimming away. Away from reality.

My past lay smothered in the deepening passion of the Jacuzzi.

I dove into the water and in doing so dove out of my present frozen waters.

My legs kept my body afloat on the surface of that cold water.

Staring at my past, I was plagued with the flow of memories unmatched elsewhere. And definitely *not* in my new environment.

Staring ahead, I found a further sauna beyond the boundaries of the Jacuzzi of my past.

I suddenly jerked my body out of the pool of my present, climbing up the shaky and unstable stairs of the pool.

Falling back at least ten times in my urgency to leave my present state of mind, I heaved a sigh of relief as I tried for the last time and landed on the ground above.

Glancing back over my shoulders, I saw the struggle as the stairs shook in response to my weight as I leveled up my body against them, trying desperately to reach the goal of my future.

Quitting was never my asset, and so I continued fighting against the grain of reform, the stairs. Conformity was a notion that I chose to discard.

I balanced my right foot on the ground outside the side of the pool, but then flipped backwards into the pool, slipping on a banana skin that erased any earlier attempts.

Choking, I swallowed water.

Struggling, I battled against the thrashing waves of my present.

Under water, I was the weakened soul; unable to breathe, I battled on.

Fighting with a might unheard of, I strangled the water, banning it from its existence in my mouth.

I was now hanging, clinging onto the edge of the swimming pool, my head choking back painful but much-needed, merciful fresh air.

Regaining my composure, I dove into the most turbulent of waters and swam away.

Stubbornness led the waves of water and, sooner rather than later, confidence became my ally.

I swam back to the staircase. And with a sudden, unexpected strength in my bones, I heaved my body up the stairs and almost ran up the three stairs, running out of the pool for dear life.

I ran away, running in the direction of my past.

I sat carefully on the edge of the Jacuzzi.

Eagerly I splashed my legs and refilled the special moments of my soul. And then, without regret, I walked out of the Jacuzzi, with bliss gripping my heart and passion left to cling to my body as droplets of a life gone by.

Exhausted, I lay on the ground, right between my bitter, harsh present and elusive past.

My eyes burned, stinging from the chlorine harshness.

Then I looked up and saw a window.

I walked toward the window slowly, throwing caution to the wind.

A peep out of the window, and I met the shooting star that collided across the beautifully dark night sky.

It was simply spectacular; the sky was littered with jewels across the night.

Stars of different shapes and sizes hung in the sky like a mirage.

Unbelievably, I saw a reflection of my face in a slow-motion shooting star.

Pronouncing the words slowly, I read:

"Go on, reach over more, much further—until the tips of your fingers hurt as they stretch out. Don't worry about the thousands of feet below you; you may just fall, and just break your fall in dreamful frenzy."

Bewildered, I stared fixedly at the night sky long after the encounter with my shooting star ended.

Feeling the urge to sit down, I found a wooden chair behind me.

Tired from my life, I got up and left.

Upon leaving the gym, I noticed that my wallet was missing—probably left on the chair.

I raced back into the gym, past the security and into the quarters of my present, past, and future.

Finding the chair, I drew to a halt and picked up my wallet.

Dusting it, the letters engraved in the chair bit into me:

"What are you waiting for? Time waits for no one."

And I knew then that Time had arrived and, walking over to the door, I opened the gates, letting him in.

# Sleeping With the Enemy (Part 8)

I took the vase, and as anger swelled in my body like a nasty bruise, I threw it at him. Not directly at him, but close enough.

"Shit! Crazy woman!" he screamed as the vase hit the wall right beside him, missing by no more than ten inches.

"You son of a bitch! You lying bastard!" I screamed, my voice shivering in anger.

"You think you can do this to me? Tell me: to me?" I pointed at my chest repeatedly in disbelief.

*Is he for real? Do I look stupid or a fool to him?* I thought to myself, trying to calm down with reason and logic.

But that's the problem right there: I never had much of either.

I ran out of the villa and slammed the front door shut with all my might.

And then, stopping short in front of my car in the garage, I looked around the area as if I was seeing it for the very first time.

And then within a minute I was behind my wheel, almost ready to run him over if I laid eyes on him just one more time.

"One more time ... just one more time," I muttered under my breath, already tired from my earlier anger outburst.

The only sentence that I kept thinking of all the way home was, "How could he do this to me? Did he hate me that much?"

*Well, did he?*

# Take Forty-four

A woman crossed the path of life.

A man waited on that path, patiently.

The woman passed him without noticing.

The man drew to a halt, surprised at the woman's absentmindedness.

She continued walking to the rhythm of her beating heart, oblivious to all that was around her.

He walked on behind her,

Walking in the path of her needs.

She walked on, still oblivious.

Suddenly, tired from her fast walk, she retired to sit on the pavement.

She was engrossed in her memories and the memories of all others around her.

He came up behind her,

And sat down right next to her.

She looked at him, into the eyes of the stranger she never knew.

He smiled into the eyes of a woman of mystery and elegance.

She turned her gaze away, staring at the path ahead of her.

He sat there next to her in silence for almost twenty minutes.

Without warning, she got up and continued on her journey.

He got up after her, amused at her constant absentmindedness.

She walked and walked.

Touring most of Central London.

He followed, seeing London from a stranger's point of view.

He borrowed her eyes as he toured London in the way she perceived it.

The woman arrived at the fountain in the heart of the West End.

She went up a step or two and settled on a step.

He climbed up the steps leading to the fountain.

He climbed right to the top and, turning his back to the fountain, threw a coin into the well of coins.

She suddenly took notice of him.

Scrutinizing him, she wondered, "What could he wish for?"

He felt her gaze settle over him.

A smile started to play on his lips as he turned to return her gaze.

He came toward her and sat again beside her.

She spoke words.

"What was your wish?" she asked rather discreetly, with a mischievous grin.

He replied, "To protect the woman next to me from absentmindedness."

She laughed.

"Who said I'm absentminded? I knew you were following me all along; I just wanted to see your persistence, how much you really wanted to speak to me. And now I stopped at the fountain because I was finally sure that after a man follows a woman he barely knows for a full day, then he really *does* want to get to know her." She winked at him as she continued telling him about herself.

He laughed at his perception of the woman beside him.

She got up to leave, and he got up with her.

This time they walked back through her tour of London, but this time he walked beside her, now seeing the city through her mind, not just her eyes.

# Sleeping With the Enemy (Part 9)

He missed her a lot—actually too much—these days.

He tried his best to keep his mind busy, to stay out with friends all the time and dive into his work, but somehow that stopped working after just one week.

Why he couldn't control his emotions and keep them at bay, he didn't understand.

After all, she wasn't the first woman nor the last one in the market. But that made absolutely no difference to him.

He loved her more today than yesterday, and with each coming day his love grew to new proportions, and that was sad because these feelings were born in the heat of her absence.

# Take Forty-five

I smiled.

And laughed.

Cried.

Giggled.

At times I held the mask of a blank, expressionless face.

But never,

Would I ever,

Dwell in the neutral warmth of safety and balance.

For that would be,

Not living,

But watching silently as life passed me by.

A lover stole my Venetian mask of a blank, expressionless face; he stole it and ripped apart his own face, gluing that mask permanently onto his face.

Watching silently from the windowsill as life passed him by.

That lover was no longer a part of me. For he lived behind a self-made, protective prison. I, on the other hand, lived amid the fields of life. He watched *those* from the comfort of his cozy chair.

Viewing life was, after all, his way of living it.

Living life was my only way.

# Take Forty-six

He ran away, his footsteps meeting the pavement with unbeatable speed.

He couldn't stop running.

Running away from the consuming personality that in turn consumed him.

Cringing, he paused on the road, heaving in a sigh of exhaustion from this personal marathon.

He held his head up high and continued his running escapade.

He ran round corners, down alleyways, and all through the areas where their love had sprung into being.

He was forced to a halt as he neared the lake in Hyde Park.

He could not run through the lake.

He would have to run all the way around the lake to the other side.

But he could not.

He would not.

Exhaustion bit into his muscles, releasing fatigue, a fatigue of the mind.

So after much thought, he decided to paddle across the lake to the other side.

Jumping in the little yellow foot-powered paddleboat, he began to pedal quickly as his mind raced against his heart.

He desperately had to reach the other side—*now*. Before he could change his mind and race into the arms of a woman he loved so dearly that it almost frightened him.

He had to rescue his heart from the only woman who knew how to nurture its growth.

Who knew subtly how to keep his heart alive with the warmth of her own.

He pedaled, forcing the boat to speed up.

His force on the pedal broke it.

He burst into tears as it dawned on him that he could not escape as easily as he had imagined.

He was now stuck in the middle of Hyde Park Lake, unable to reach his escape and also unable to reach his love.

Just stuck in the middle.

Without his knowledge, God had placed him there on purpose.

God had created a lake, interrupting his escapade; God had created his will to take the shortcut by paddling across the lake; God had even pulled the wool over his eyes to stop him from seeing any other alternatives.

He sat there in the little boat as it rocked back and forth on the lake.

He found himself relaxing as the boat rocked him back and forth, now a baby in his mother's arms.

His thoughts haunted him, not allowing his mind or heart to rock blissfully to sleep.

He closed his eyes, desperately escaping into the land of his dreams.

But God had other plans for him.

She came into his mind, overpowering him with the wealth of memories of happiness, of sexual ecstasy, of comfort in his arms.

He felt himself breaking into a large smile that threatened to overshadow his face.

He lay down on the floor of the boat and stared into the sky that had gradually fallen into darkness.

He found the breeze whisking a memory and flying it to the corners of his head.

The memory was that of lovers in a park, talking, chatting, staring into nothingness, and taking part in sexual endearments.

That was when he realized.

He had run away to their place.

Ironically, he was so frightened he had only concentrated on escaping from that woman; he forgot that what he had done was run into her arms *again*.

He had escaped the physical imprint of her arms but found himself smack in the middle of her environment.

Her arms theoretically surrounded Hyde Park, creating a well of memories.

And he was now in that well, that lake of memories.

He cried for the second time in his life.

Crying because he had almost lost the only woman who had defined love through loving him.

He got up and, to his dismay, found himself right next to the shore he had wished to cross earlier.

He got out of the boat.

Walking around the wrong side, he called her, asking her to join him.

Before he could end that two-minute phone call, he suddenly tripped over someone lurking in the dark.

He screamed.

The woman got up, throwing him off quite suddenly where he had landed.

He had landed on her.

She also screamed, frightened in the dark.

Until their eyes settled on each other.

The man lay aghast; the woman, shocked.

She smiled as he took in that woman who made his heart come alive with her presence.

He took her for a stroll down memory lane.

And finally giving up, he admitted his love at the end of their walk.

God had interfered and was now busy smiling upon them.

# Sleeping With the Enemy (Part 10)

It was a relief. The very best kind.

The kind that wakes you up every morning with a happy state of mind. The kind that makes you feel like you had just gotten away in the nick of time.

She was a burglar, alright. She stole his heart without permission and continued planning her escape with it.

Even when he told her that other women before her had tried to do the exact same thing, it never made a dent anyway.

It was the most beautiful crime she had ever committed. A crime that left him in a heap on the floor.

He fell alright, but exactly how much he missed her she would never know.

How could she find out? To make a robbery successful you had to cut away from all the people who were involved in your escapade, especially the ornament that you stole. You could not keep your most prized possession.

So you spent your days marveling at your plan: your wit and intelligence, and the wool that you pulled over his eyes.

It was a scam, and the result was just magnificent.

She stole his heart and would never return it. But she reminded herself why she had: simply because she had to teach him what it meant to break another's heart in two or neglect another's feelings for your own. In a nutshell, she had to teach him what he had been doing to all the women who had entered his life before her.

And somehow, one way or the other, she felt and knew deep down inside her heart of all hearts that she had succeeded.

And that, she reminded herself, was more than enough.

# Take Forty-seven

I stood outside, shielded in the striking cold of London.

Mesmerized in the absence of a lover.

Fidgeting, I stood, unsure of the action needed from me.

Thoughts ran along the outskirts of my mind.

He had not called.

He had not promised to call, but either way, he should've called.

The night of sexual passion remained the backdrop of any expectations.

Staring blindly ahead, I stood.

I dove into the puddle of curiosity.

Curiosity attacked my clothes with its droplets of confusion.

Insane, I tripped over the sanity of my mind in my desperate attempt to find out the main reason of his absence.

But that I would never know.

I broke out into a smile of knowledge, a smile trapped in the reality of a frown.

I should have known better.

Last night I dove into the body that possessed the soul of my past.

Drinking, sharing, giving and receiving erotically.

He had approached my sacred temple, teasing it into submission.

Teaching me the wonders of the human sex, the sensual touches of a man intoxicated with sexual fervor.

And I had melted over the body of a man of intolerable sexuality.

His touches, subtle yet demanding, sent my body earth-quaking into spasms.

Smiling, my frown escaped.

After all, a night to remember is much better than a night imagined.

And he had given me the priceless gift of a memory.

I no longer waited for his call, and when it came, I never picked up.

Why would I risk ruining such a perfect memory with more interactions?

# Take Forty-eight

He smiled, a half-broken smile, broken by the increasing tension and pressure that he applied. He was trying to challenge himself into the role of a man, an experienced one. The challenge bore its glow on his lover's face as she squirmed in pain. The only pain that crowned her with a refreshing glow of beauty, that set her face alight with a passion she had only dreamed of before.

It was a pain that would finally release upon her the electrifying dosage of womanhood. She smiled as the pain increased in its intensity and momentum, for she knew then, at that exact moment, that pain was indeed her one and only pleasure.

He gave birth to a well of fire between her legs, and it was then that she felt unnecessary doubt cast its shadow over her. As the first flame met her barrier, she muttered, "There's nowhere for you to go … it's not going to break …"

A sudden push from her lover and she was greeted by the man with a frown, the man of pain. Squirming against the threshold of the bed, her head played a rhythm of drums against the headboard.

Beating her head repeatedly against the headboard channeled an increasing intensity in between her legs. Heaving in and out, a sudden burst of pain and heat exploded down her thighs in anticipation and preparation of what was about to happen only seconds later.

She focused on the eyes of her lover as they began telling a story she had waited all her life to hear and experience.

His eyes told the story of a man and his woman sustaining a love, the unexpected kind.

His tears signaled a path down the slopes of his face.

She grabbed hard onto the back of the headboard, digging in her nails with a hard grip on the board, to elevate the pain that would arrive sooner than she had ever imagined.

And then she felt him.

She felt the power of his manhood surge into her own being.

Three of her nails broke on the headboard as she gripped it, not knowing how painful this could get.

Releasing her grip from the headboard, she held onto his upper arms and began feeling sensations very foreign to her.

Suddenly, all her senses—sight, touch, and scent; the sound of her pleasure and the moment—all collided together to move in harmony.

It was the very first time that all her senses were in tune with her body and his at once. An increasingly sharp, heightened collection of senses made every part of her body come alive in a way that she never thought possible.

He entered, moving very slowly in the woman he had always loved and would love for the remainder of his days, or so she had hoped.

She could feel his every move. Even when he didn't move inside of her, she could feel when he slightly tilted to the right. Unknown to him, she felt him in every possible way and was intertwined by a cable to his movements, his very being, with an increasingly high dosage and volume, even bass.

He started moving slowly, then faster; suddenly it was a burst of intense pleasure that was as uncomfortable as it was electrifying.

Her eyes filled with tears as his words hit home in her heart. They spent the next two hours in each other's arms in bed, sleeping.

# Sleeping With the Enemy
# (Part 11)

And so it was a story of a man of deceit, a man who led and preached to groups of men, teaching them, guiding them on the basics of how to charm the women of their desires.

A man many looked up to, a playboy if you will, a charmer and a king in women's land.

What a pity that that king was overthrown, and in his place a woman set the world in the right order.

# Take Forty-nine

She never knew why or when it had happened. She only knew the moment that it had all fallen into place ... that moment that she had met her man. It was perhaps destiny that had brought him so readily to her door. Fate that had held her hand and typed the very first e-mail. What followed was a love story in all its glory.

She found herself in his e-mails and at many times in his words. As he spoke of his ambition and dream in life, she saw hers mirrored in his. She realized that with each e-mail there was a special language growing in between their words. A language that they only understood.

Her days and nights were spent in the warmth and glow of his presence in her life. He had managed to find himself in her. He saw a new side of himself in her eyes. She was the only person who had ever truly understood the threads that were so closely intertwined in his heart. And he had loved her for it.

His face spoke a silent dialogue with hers. Telepathy was an art that they had both mastered together. Or perhaps it was just a matter of a love that knew no boundaries or obstacles.

He was a man who had entered her life stealthily and bestowed upon her the most beautiful moments of her life. He taught her the definition of support and showed her in so many ways what it really meant to love a woman. He spent his days thinking of ways to enrich her life and showered her with a love that was only found in the world's best classics and films.

Indeed, it was a love that all were in awe off. Others around them were bewildered at the love that they themselves never felt.

He crowned her with a love that knew no limits, and in return she chose to honor their love, christening him and only him with her very soul. She made love to him as she had always dreamed. Deep in her soul, she felt the time had come for her to experience the act of making love with the only man she had truly loved. It was one of the most magical moments in her life. She had always wondered, *When the time came, would it ever be as perfect?*

And she was lucky … it was as perfect as she had always imagined her first time would be.

She knew deep inside her heart that that moment was as special to him as it had been for her. Even today, she can close her eyes and remember the very seconds that they had spent in her threshold. She saw the eagerness in his eyes, the love that sparkled in response to her very own. The tenderness that manifested itself over them.

The genuine seriousness of the very moment that transformed them into adulthood.

They had spent a many blissful nights and days, strolling in and out of life's every situation. Laughing, crying, and dancing to the beats of their hearts, which in time became one and the same heart.

Drinking sake and eating salmon sashimi, they quietly retired from their fast-paced lives to spend silent moments together, speaking about everything and nothing at all. The true test of their love lay in the fact that they loved simply being silent together.

Then one day, the man she had almost lived with for so long was nowhere to be found. In his place, she found a new man, one she neither understands nor ever wanted to. A stranger had taken his place, and in her sorrow she lost the man she had bonded with in ways that no one could ever understand. With a click of a finger, he had been kidnapped.

She knew that he was brainwashing himself in a daily shower, and he had finally succeeded. He had gotten himself to believe that this very woman was a woman he could never trust and no longer loved. She knew he was in pain, because in reality and deep down inside, she knew that a leopard never changed its spots.

She wanted to hate the man who had ironically taught her the meaning of love and hate in different fluttering seasonal moments.

But she was not a resentful woman who spent her life with hatred. She was different. She would always remain true to herself. She did not need to react to such inflictions of pain from the very person who in the past had spent endless nights protecting her.

She could not hate a man she had once loved so deeply. To her, at least, that remained impossible …

How he had done it she would never understand …

But as in all love stories, one part of the person always changes. It's as simple as that. Today she smiles when she thinks of one of life's greatest love affairs.

And then she is reminded how lucky she was to experience such a unique affair and how she had always been lucky in love with others before him.

She wanted him to know—needed him to know—that she still admired him, although life's circumstances would always keep them apart. She understood that he valued family above all; after all, she did too. But in life's most joyful of moments—and she's had many since he escaped her life—he would overshadow her thoughts for a second or two. She would think: "I hope that he gets to enjoy life as much as I am at this moment, because of all the people I know, he's the only one who truly deserves it."

And a snap and crackle later, she is laughing and dancing like never before.

It was a love that called to her on the sunny day of June 1994 and a love that lost its voice in the spring leaves of 1996. She patched up her voice and continued.

# Sleeping With the Enemy (Final)

From where she was crowned, from where she reigned, through the looking glass, she watched him. Almost daily and in her solitude, she would awake at night to stare at his life for a couple of minutes or so before she returned to hers.

But that was harmless.

Or so she had hoped. To know that out there was a man unlike any other, who was able to communicate with the strands that held her physical desires together. To shorten them, tie them, extend them, and cut them—exactly where needed, and in response to her body's needs and in its earth-shattering ways.

In simple terms: he molded her world.

He designed the physical world that she held daily in the grasp of her palms—needless to say, turning it into a frenzy.

And today she missed his hold over her world.

But tomorrow she would find another.

Again, simplicity was yet another order.

# Take Fifty

Who's that person?

The woman who walks through the roads, streets, and alleyways, and then stops at cafés and laughs with friends at everything and nothing at all, all at once?

Who's that person?

That man who walks every corner and pauses before he starts whistling to his favorite song and drumming his knuckles and fingers on pavement posts?

Who's that person?

That kid that laughs and cries, forgetting the difference between the two?

Who's that person?

The surgeon that takes every man's nagging ache and physique on a serious note, that man who wears black and all its darker, brotherly shades: navy blue, dark gray, and even the darkest gray?

Who's that person?

The mother who sees only her children magnified, up close and personal, answering their every whimper with surrender?

Who's that person?

Your colleague that carefully peers over your shoulders, trading your tricks of the trade for his or her own and then smiling, yet enjoying daily lunch with you?

Who's that person?

Your aunt, uncle, or relative in neutral or extended family woes who has taught you the secret of success: your ultimate belief in yourself. Lucky is one who finds such a match. I know I have.

Who's that person?

The reader that lives the lives of writers everywhere, escaping his or her own life for a Kit Kat or a much-needed caffeine break?

Who's that person?

The father who makes all life's challenges possible because in doing so he prepares you for the greatest of life's challenges: knowing thyself.

Who's that person?

The writer of this book? The men and women of all takes? The characters that spin this story out of control? The writer? Who's that person? A person who watches everybody as they go on daily interacting with others, who laughs at the simplest of details, who marvels at creations before them on cinema screens, in theaters, in scripts, and in life as it unfolds in front of them? Writers, and what a curious bunch they are!

Who's that person?

You—as you read all the words before you on one page and endless others, interpreting them in your own way. *You, for whom I write the stories. Just you.*